PLAYING WITH SEDUCTION

THE PLAYERS CLUB
BOOK THREE

ERIKA WILDE

PLAYING WITH SEDUCTION

One unexpected photoshoot. One irresistible younger man. One chance to believe in love again.

I love my work as a boudoir photographer. Helping women see their confidence and beauty through my lens is the most rewarding part of my career. When I hire Jase Burns—a dangerously handsome model—to pose for a custom romance novel cover shoot, I'm unprepared for the attraction between us.

After a painful divorce, trusting any man feels risky...especially one who's eight years younger and far too charming for my peace of mind. I try to keep my distance, convinced our lives are moving in different directions. But Jase isn't easily discouraged, and his steady confidence slowly chips away at the walls around my heart.

One unforgettable night at The Players Club changes everything, revealing a connection that feels deeper than either of us expected. Now the man I once tried to resist is the one making me question every rule I set for myself.

Playing with Seduction is a heartfelt contemporary romance featuring a confident heroine, a determined younger hero, age-gap tension, emotional healing after heartbreak, and a passionate love story set in the exclusive world of The Players Club.

CHAPTER 1

Kendall

"*H*oly shit. Did the temperature just rise in here, or am I having a premature hot flash?"

I laughed at my friend's tongue-in-cheek comment, along with the dramatic way she fanned her face with her hand. I knew Stephanie Randall wasn't alluding to menopause but rather the gorgeous, sexy guy who'd just walked into Pure Bliss Boudoir Photography.

Yes, Jase Burns *was* the epitome of hot.

Everything about him radiated the kind of sweltering heat that made a woman—me especially—soften and melt in all the right places. And that was with him fully dressed. Once he peeled away his shirt and jeans and I had free access to stare at his perfectly sculpted body, it was difficult to keep my mouth from watering and my sorely neglected female parts from perking up, as well.

He was heading our way, where I was getting my equipment ready for the photo shoot Jase had arrived for—which was why Stephanie was there in the first place. My friend's business in creating fantasy bedrooms for clients came in handy for my various boudoir displays. And in this case, she'd helped set up a seductive setting for the romance novel cover shoot a bestselling author had hired me to do.

Jase's stride was confident as he approached us, his dark, chocolate-brown eyes solely focused on me. The light stubble along his jawline and chin, which my client had requested for this particular series of photographs, was distracting as hell, because it made me wonder how it would feel to have that light dusting of facial hair abrading my neck, across my breasts, between my thighs...

I swallowed back a moan at the thought, even as my inner hussy responded to the erotic images filling my head. *Yeah, let the melting commence.*

"Hey, sweetheart," Jase drawled, greeting me with the pet name he'd given me and a smile that hinted at all kinds of sin. "This is the third time you've had me back. If you can't get enough, all you have to do is say yes to going out on a date with me, and I'm all yours."

I bit the inside of my cheek to keep from returning his smile. The man was absolutely shameless. A charming, gorgeous, persistent flirt who wasn't the least bit deterred by my many rejections, despite my excuse that I didn't mix business with pleasure. No, my reasons for turning down Jase in particular ran much deeper and were based on my personal hang-ups, courtesy of the way my ex-husband, Drew, had blind-sided me with the end of our marriage.

"It's all about what the client wants," I said in a light, teasing voice, aware of the fact that

Stephanie was watching the exchange with interest. "You know that."

He tipped his head slightly and arched a light brown eyebrow. "But what about what *you* want?"

I tried not to think about what I wanted with a guy like Jase, because it was all X-rated and belonged in my bedroom—when I was *alone* at night and could indulge in those wicked fantasies that, lately, always starred *him*.

When I didn't reply, Jase shifted his gaze to Stephanie. The two had never met before, and he flashed her a dazzling grin before introducing himself. "I'm Jase Burns."

"Nice to meet you." Stephanie's eyes twinkled mischievously as she slid her hand into the bigger one he'd extended her way. "I'm Kendall's *very* good friend, Stephanie."

"As Kendall's *very* good friend, don't you think she ought to give me a chance?" he said without missing a beat. "I'm really a nice guy. I'm former military and I work for Noble and Associates as a security analyst, so you know I'm not some crazy stalker."

My jaw nearly dropped open. I couldn't believe he was enlisting Stephanie's help in persuading me, and I so didn't trust the sudden look of commiseration on my friend's face.

"I absolutely agree she should give you a chance," Stephanie said, laughter in her voice. "She desperately needs to loosen up and have some fun."

Before Jase could respond to the fact that Stephanie had just unintentionally labeled me as boring and mundane, which was something that still had the ability to make my stomach twist with stupid insecurities, I changed the subject.

"Nicole is already in one of the dressing rooms getting ready," I said, my tone all business, which I decided was the best way to handle Jase. "You can do the same. I need you to strip down to just your black briefs for today's photo shoot, per the author's request."

"You got it," he replied, then turned his friendly gaze to Stephanie. "I hope to see you again."

"Same here," Stephanie replied, then watched as Jase walked away, his backside just as toned and gorgeous as the front. She waited until he'd disappeared into the adjoining studio that was set up like a bedroom scene, and was out of hearing range, before glancing back at me with a look of disbelief.

"Have you lost your mind?" Stephanie asked in a low, incredulous tone of voice. "How can you say no to *that*? The man is sex on a stick, and those seductive brown eyes of his were all but eating you up."

My friend's choice of words singed my brain with a carnal vision of all the ways he could *eat me up*. "Saying no is easy," I said with a nonchalant shrug that belied my undeniable attraction to Jase. "He's twenty-seven and way too young for me." As I was thirty-five, that was an eight-year age difference between us that couldn't be wider. A younger man like Jase would no doubt move on as soon as he got what he wanted from me. Been there, done that, and had the emotional scars and divorce papers to prove it.

Stephanie waggled her brows lasciviously. "All I have to say to that is lots and lots of stamina."

Sadly, stamina when it came to sex was a concept that was totally foreign to me. The one and only man I'd ever slept with, then was married to for nearly ten years, lacked staying power in the bedroom. I didn't have anything to compare to, but Drew hadn't been one for hot, sweaty, passionate trysts. He'd been more of a missionary kind of guy, and once he climaxed, he'd roll over to his side of the bed and fall asleep. That had been my normal, and even those quick, less-than-satisfying encounters had dwindled down to an obligatory screw during the last two years of our marriage.

"As you can see, he's a huge flirt and probably a player," I said as I pulled out a drawer to find a memory card for my camera. "And that's the last thing I'm interested in."

Stephanie smirked. "Yeah, well, how's that Internet dating thing working out for you?"

I didn't miss the sarcasm lacing my friend's voice. Yes, I'd just recently decided to join an online matchmaking service. After two years of being single, I was ready to dip my toe back into the dating pool, but in a way that provided me with eligible men who shared the same goals in life that I did. Despite my divorce, I was still the kind of woman who preferred being in a stable, committed relationship. More than anything, I wanted to be happily married with a family, and thought by now I'd have at least two kids, if not more. My biological clock was ticking louder by the day.

"It's working out just fine," I said as I changed the lens on my camera. "Grant is out of town on business right now, but I have a third date with him next Thursday night."

"The chiropractor guy?" Stephanie wrinkled her nose.

"Yes, the chiropractor guy," I mocked right back. "We actually have a lot in common. He's my age, we have the same political views, we enjoy the same kind of music and books, and he's looking for a serious relationship that could lead to more." For me, that was the beauty of an online dating site. The extensive compatibility and personality tests I'd had to fill out ensured I wasn't wasting my time with someone unsuitable.

Stephanie feigned a bored yawn. "Yeah, yeah, so chiropractor guy likes and wants all the same things that you do. That's great. Have you slept with him yet?"

"No. We've only been out twice."

"Fair enough," her friend conceded but didn't let up. "Let me rephrase my question. Do you *want* to sleep with him?"

I opened my mouth, then quickly shut it again, realizing I couldn't answer Stephanie with the enthusiastic *yes* my friend was looking for. "Dating Grant isn't about sex. We're taking it slow and getting to know one another. We're not even exclusive yet." I figured that desire would happen organically, over time. That's just the way it seemed to work for me and my body's libido. Except I couldn't help but notice that when it came to Jase, my body always seemed raring to go.

"You didn't answer my question," Stephanie went on relentlessly as she crossed her arms over her chest. "Do you want to rip off his clothes and drop to your knees to get up close and personal with his cock? When you look at chiropractor guy, do your girly parts get all warm and tingly because you can't stop thinking about getting down and dirty with him?"

"Yes, yes, I'm attracted to him," I said with a laugh, giving Stephanie what she wanted to hear. And I *did* find Grant attractive. He was classically handsome, with warm green eyes and an easy smile. He liked running every day and had a nice body to show for it. He was a gentleman, and though we'd only kissed once on our last date, I'd enjoyed it.

Stephanie sighed and didn't look convinced. "Finding Grant *attractive* and compatible is all well and good, but what about passion and lust?"

I settled the camera strap around my neck, a safety precaution just in case it slipped from my hands during the photo shoot, and decided to be honest—with my friend, and myself. "Passion and lust isn't something I've had a whole lot of experience with. Maybe I'm just not the kind of woman who gets all worked up over sex." Or the kind of woman who made men go wild with the uncontrollable need to pin me to the nearest mattress and take me hard, fast, and a bit on the rough side. No, that was a fantasy that would probably never become a reality.

"Let me tell you something," Stephanie said, her brows creased in a suddenly serious expression. "After what your dirty, lying, cheating, pencil-dick of an ex-husband did to you, you *deserve* a man who will make you feel those things. And you know that the girls would agree with me."

Oh, yeah, they would. The girls—Raina, Paige, Jillian, and Summer, who were all a part of our monthly girls' night out group—would undoubtedly back up Stephanie. Especially Raina, Paige, and Jillian, who had men in their lives who made sure their women were well satisfied in the bedroom.

"How about we save the rest of this conversation for our next get-together?" I said, not wanting to talk about my love life, or lack thereof, any longer. "Some of us have work to do."

"I *am* working," Stephanie said, sounding slightly affronted. "I brought you that new comforter and draping for the bedroom scene you're shooting today, didn't I?"

"Yes, you did, thank you very much." I appreciated my friend's help, as well as Stephanie's eye for design. "It's exactly what the author wanted."

Jase strolled out of the studio area at that moment, wearing nothing but his tight black briefs—just as I had instructed—and it took extreme effort for me to keep my eyes *above* his chest so he didn't catch me staring at those tight abs and the outline of his man parts. I could do plenty of ogling and fantasizing from behind my camera, and again when I edited the batch of pictures on my computer.

"Nicole and I are ready when you are," he said, hooking his thumb over his shoulder toward the studio.

"Be right there," I said as I grabbed an extra battery pack.

He returned to the adjoining room, and Stephanie leaned toward me and whispered, "*Dayum*, you *really* need to tap that."

I just shook my head and didn't respond, because tapping anything of Jase's wasn't going to happen.

"Can I at least stay and watch the photo shoot?" Stephanie asked, much too eagerly.

"No." I would never be able to concentrate with my friend popping off with inappropriate and sexual comments.

Stephanie made a face at me. "Spoil sport. Try and at least enjoy the eye candy."

Looking but no touching. "That I can do," I said with a smile. "I'll see you later."

"Yes, you will."

Stephanie walked out of the building, and with a deep breath, I headed into the studio room that had been transformed into an elegant boudoir, complete with a cream-colored silk chaise lounge, a vanity set with a mirror and cushioned chair, and a large four-poster bed as the main centerpiece in the plush room. I used this setting often for my female clients and had recently started taking on couples who wanted more intimate photos taken of them together, as well.

This was Jase and Nicole's third, and last, session together as cover models—thank goodness. I had already provided my author client with shots of Jase and Nicole getting sexy on a big, executive-type desk, and the second time had been about capturing the two of them going at each other hot and heavy up against the wall. Today, the author had requested a bedroom backdrop and wanted this cover photo to be the hottest one yet. Erotic and male-dominated had been the description she'd used over the phone.

The couple was standing off to the side, waiting for my instructions—Jase in his inde-cently tight black briefs and Nicole in a black silky camisole that barely covered her surgi-cally enhanced boobs and matching lace panties. The younger girl had a great body—a tiny waist and hips and long, slender legs—and her waist-length blonde hair had been styled into soft curls that fell over her shoulders. She was gorgeous, and together they made a stunning couple, in person and in photos.

"Okay, guys, I need you two up on the middle of the bed, with Nicole on the bottom and Jase on top," I said as I focused on setting up the lighting in the room, which gave them plenty of time to get situated on the mattress.

When I turned back around, Jase and Nicole were in a classic horizontal position with him positioned between the girls' thighs and were ready to get started. I heard Jase murmur something to Nicole that made the young girl laugh, and my stomach gave a little twist that felt too much like a pang of jealousy.

What the hell? Mortified by the unexpected feeling, I shook it off and reminded myself that I did this *all the time* with couples and always remained professional.

This session was no different. Or so I tried to convince myself.

"For this photo shoot, I need a lot of passion and lust," I said, repeating what the client had asked for. "Jase, I need you to be more assertive with Nicole in these photos."

He turned his head and flashed me a seductive bad-boy grin. "So, you want it more aggressive?"

His comment, asked oh-so-innocently, was anything but. The heat in his eyes was aimed right at me, his tempting words meant for me and me alone, despite the other woman pinned beneath him.

I swallowed to ease the sudden dryness in my mouth. "Yes, that would be great."

I lifted my camera and got to work—and so did Jase and Nicole. I had to admit the two of them had great chemistry together and followed my direction for hand placement, emotion, and suggested positions with ease. Then again, Nicole had already made it clear in previous sessions that she was interested in Jase, so I supposed that writhing beneath his strong, hard body and arching her neck so he could skim his lips along her throat was no hardship for the other woman.

Jase didn't disappoint in the assertive department, either, and slipped into that dominant role as if it came naturally to him. The expression on his face was pure alpha male as he wrapped Nicole's long hair around his fist, and when the girl's hands began drifting down over his ass, he grabbed her wrists and secured them over her head, which made for a provocative snapshot. Nicole's lips parted on a gasp, and this time I couldn't deny the streak of envy that gripped me—or the pulse of heat that settled between my thighs.

I'd never felt like a voyeur during one of my sessions, but I did now. As I caught all that eroticism on film and watched Jase in such a sexual situation, even if it was all acting, it caused a wave of arousal to seep through my veins. A restless ache swirled in my belly, my nipples tightened into hard points, and my skin felt warm—everywhere.

Good God, I felt as though I were going to spontaneously combust and couldn't remember the last time I'd been so turned on. Even with my ex-husband, his form of quick foreplay hadn't even come close to igniting my desire the way just *watching* Jase did, even if it was from behind a camera lens. But being a peeping Tom and getting all hot and bothered by Jase was beginning to make me feel depraved, and very deprived.

I exhaled a deep breath that did little to smother the lust that had me so off-balance, mentally *and* physically. I needed to get a grip, and after taking a moment to pretend as though I were checking the digital files on the camera's viewfinder, I returned my attention to the couple on the bed.

All I had to do was get through this last photo session, and then the temptation that was Jase Burns would no longer be a crazy sexual distraction in my life. It was a thought that both relieved and disappointed me.

CHAPTER 2

Jase

I couldn't remember a time when I'd fantasized about another woman while I had a very warm and willing one writhing beneath me. I guessed there was a first time for everything, because even though Nicole had made it verbally and physically clear that she was attracted to me, and was currently rubbing against me like a cat in heat, my thoughts were on the sexy woman standing next to the bed taking pictures of the two of us acting as though we were in the throes of passion.

At least *I* was pretending. Nicole, however, was putting on a very convincing performance. Her spread thighs gripped my hips while she arched her back and rocked her lower body against mine, then rubbed her lace-covered breasts across my chest. Her eyes were heavy lidded, and her glossy lips were parted as she panted for breath. Every time I dared to lower my head to give Kendall the more erotic shot she'd asked for, Nicole tipped her mouth up to mine for a kiss, which I'd so far managed to avoid.

I thought keeping Nicole pinned beneath me with her hands locked above her head would give me more control of the situation and her grinding movements, but she was clearly a girl who liked to be wild and in control herself. Somewhere along the way, it was as if she'd forgotten that Kendall was taking photos for a romance novel cover and that none of this was real.

I closed my eyes and clenched my jaw, knowing it didn't help matters that the long legs locked around my waist kept me strategically positioned between Nicole's thighs for maximum pressure and friction. *Shit.* I was a red-blooded man, and I wasn't immune to Nicole's enthusiastic response, even though it was Kendall that I fantasized about having restrained and moaning beneath me.

Moaning *and* shuddering, I realized as I opened my eyes and saw Nicole's increasingly rapturous expression. She was in her own little erotic world, and *Jesus Christ*, if Kendall didn't end this session very soon, she was going to capture Nicole's orgasm on film for prosperity.

"Great job, you two," Kendall finally said, her voice huskier than I had ever heard it before—as if this session had quite possibly turned her on, as well. "I got some amazing shots that the author is going to love, so I think we're finished."

Thank fucking God. I couldn't scramble off of Nicole quickly enough, though it did take the other woman a few extra moments to realize that the photo session was over. The haze in her eyes gradually cleared, leaving behind a look of disappointment as she frowned at me. I'd never left a woman unsatisfied before—another first—but I just wasn't interested in Nicole, despite her attempts to entice me.

Kendall, on the other hand, wouldn't even look my way as she fiddled with the settings on her camera, but there was no mistaking the warm flush on her face or the tight nipples pressing against the silky tank top she was wearing.

"Go ahead and get dressed, and I'll meet you two out front," Kendall said, then quickly disappeared from the bedroom area, leaving me alone to deal with Nicole.

I grabbed my jeans and quickly put them on as Nicole slid off the bed. She gave me a sultry smile and skimmed her index finger down my chest, along the groove bisecting my abs, and tucked it into the waistband of my pants.

"Such a shame to let all that foreplay go to waste," she said, stepping closer so her breasts deliberately brushed against my bare chest. "My place isn't far from here if you're interested in finishing what we started."

I took a step back, dislodging her hand from the fly of my jeans, and summoned a regretful look. Nicole was a nice girl, but if I was going to spend the evening with anyone, I wanted it to be with the stubborn, headstrong woman in the other room.

Yeah, good luck with that, my mind taunted, considering she'd already turned me down the four other times I'd asked her out on a date.

"I'm really sorry, but I already have other plans," I lied, trying to let her down easy. Even if I didn't get what I wanted from Kendall, hooking up with Nicole held no appeal to me.

Nicole's lip plumped out in a pout. "Too bad," she said with a sigh, then turned and headed to the dressing area to put her clothes on.

I didn't miss the extra sway in her hips or the way she glanced over her shoulder with an *it's your loss* kind of look. I was certain any other guy would be chasing right after her, but over the past year or so, I'd grown more discriminating when it came to women.

After eight years in the Air Force, and a string of flighty one-night stands because anything more didn't mesh with my on-the-go lifestyle, I now wanted something more than just easy, casual sex. I wanted a mature woman I could actually have an intelligent conversation with. Someone confident and settled, in her life and career. And one who was experienced enough sexually to not only accept my preference for control in the bedroom but enjoy it as well. For me, that type of elevated sexual play took trust, along with an explicit intimacy that didn't exist in the quick, scratch-my-itch kind of sex that Nicole was offering.

I put my T-shirt back on, along with my socks and shoes. Finished dressing, I strolled out to the front area of the studio, where Kendall was standing at a counter downloading the photos she'd just taken onto her laptop. I'd met her about a month ago at a wedding reception where I'd been working security. I'd taken one look at her in the sexy black gown she'd been wearing, and for me it had been *I want you* at first sight. For her, it had been *I want you as a cover model* at first sight.

Yeah, our personal agendas had conflicted slightly, and since she'd flat-out turned me down for a date, my only option to continue seeing her was to agree to the modeling gig. Unfortunately, she remained steadfast in her resolve to keep things strictly professional between us.

I came up beside her to get a better look at

the pictures, and my arm brushed along hers. I heard a tiny intake of breath as she subtly shifted away from me. There was no denying the spark of awareness between us, though she definitely did her best to *not* acknowledge the sexual tension in any way. Which only made me more determined to shake up her too prim and proper composure.

"You two photograph well together," she said in a light, breezy tone as she scrolled through the shots, attempting to keep things casual between us. "You're stunning as a couple, and Nicole is totally into you."

I got the impression that Kendall was actually *encouraging* me to date Nicole—which made my gut burn with frustration. "It's all one-sided."

"Didn't look that way to me," she teased, just as a very erotic and suggestive photograph filled her screen that made a mockery of my words.

I opened my mouth to tell her exactly what carnal thoughts had filled my head while Nicole had been squirming beneath me with her legs wrapped around my waist, but didn't get the chance as the other woman walked out of the bedroom studio to join us. She was dressed in an indecently high miniskirt and a tight, low-cut blouse that exposed nearly half of her breasts.

"Here's your fee for today's session," Kendall said with a smile and handed Nicole a check.

"Thanks. It's been fun." Nicole slipped the check into her purse, then gave me a blatant once-over while licking her bottom lip. "You sure I can't convince you to come over to my place for a few hours?"

Annoyance swept through me, that Nicole would be so brazen in front of Kendall when I'd already, very nicely, turned her down. I shook my head. "No. My plans haven't changed."

"All right, then. I guess I'm on my own," she said meaningfully and gave us both a little finger wave before walking out of the studio.

Once she was gone, Kendall glanced at me with a half smile. "You do realize, don't you, that you just turned down a sure thing?"

What the hell was up with her pushing me toward another woman? "That was way too easy," I said about Nicole. I leaned a hip against the high countertop while pinning her with my direct gaze. "I like a bit of a challenge when it comes to the woman I'm interested in." Kendall had certainly provided that.

She laughed lightly. "You're a glutton for rejection, aren't you?"

"It's a good thing I don't have a big ego," I said with a shrug. "Have dinner with me tonight. Any night. You choose the day and time."

Her lips flattened, and her green eyes turned serious. "Jase, you're a really nice guy, but I think we'd be better off as friends."

God, I *hated* being shoved into the friend zone. Especially with her. "Why just friends?" I asked, crossing my arms over my chest. "I'm attracted to you. You're attracted to me. We're both single. I'm just asking you out on a date, not to marry me," I joked.

She tensed at the comment, clearly uptight about something I'd said.

I softened my tone and tried a different approach. "Give me a legitimate reason you won't give me chance, and I'll back off."

She exhaled a deep breath. "First of all, I'm divorced."

I feigned a shocked look. "Oooh, the scandal," I teased.

She didn't so much as crack a smile. "And I'm thirty-five, and you're twenty-seven. That's an eight-year age difference between us."

I already knew how old she was, thanks to Sawyer's girlfriend, Paige, who was also one of Kendall's closest friends. Since her age had never been an issue for me, it hadn't even occurred to me that it would be a deal breaker for her. I was actually surprised she'd used the age difference as an excuse, but before my mind could come up with a practical counterargument, she picked up a check from the counter and handed it to me.

"I appreciate you agreeing to model for the cover of my client's book, and here's your final payment for your time."

Was she fucking serious? I glanced from the check to her dignified expression, and yeah, she was fucking serious. "I don't need the money," I said, the low, frustrated growl of my voice vibrating in my chest. "The only reason I'm here is because of *you*. I'm taking major shit from the guys at work because I'm going to be on the cover of some romance novel, when all I want is for you to give me, and this attraction between us, a chance."

"I'm sorry," she said softly.

It wasn't an apology I wanted, not when I knew she was fighting the heat and desire we'd both been feeling since the day we'd met. I took a slow step forward, then another, deliberately crowding her against the countertop and bracing my hands on the edge on either side of her body.

Her lips parted, and one word from her —*wait, stop, no*—and I would have respected her request and backed off immediately. But instead, I saw a flicker of anticipation in her gaze that contradicted everything she'd said up to this point. She wanted me just as much as I craved her, and that undeniable knowledge was all I needed to make a split-second decision I hoped I didn't come to regret.

Lifting a hand, I slid my palm around to the nape of her neck and used my thumb to tip her chin up higher, so that her mouth was more accessible and right beneath mine. She stared up at me with wide eyes that had darkened from a light green to a richer shade of moss. Again, no verbal protest from her, and the telltale rise and fall of her chest spurred me on.

"Let's see what I can do to convince you to change your mind," I murmured and gave in to the overwhelming need to kiss her.

The moment my mouth covered hers, she stiffened and her hands flattened against my chest, but she didn't push me away like I expected. Instead, her fingers curled into my T-shirt and she moaned softly, as if resisting me was futile. Her lips were soft, pliant, and another tiny sound caught in her throat when I swept my tongue inside and stroked along hers. One taste of Kendall and I was desperate for more. The primitive urge to claim this woman surged through me like a wild current, and I deepened the kiss, pulling her into the hot, dark wanting right along with me.

As if I'd awakened something dormant inside her, she came along willingly. Even when my mouth turned aggressive and demanding, she let me sate my hunger. The flavor of her was so damn addicting, her acquiescence so instinctive, that I knew no other woman would satisfy me the same way. I fisted the hair at the nape of her neck in my fingers to keep her mouth secured beneath mine as I pushed my hips against hers, making sure she felt just how fucking hard she made me. And how much I wanted her.

Certain I'd given her plenty of irrefutable evidence to prove our mutual attraction, I lifted my mouth from hers and took in her damp, parted lips and dazed expression. Her lashes fluttered open, her dark eyes revealing a combination of lust and desire that pleased me immensely.

I smiled confidently and skimmed my thumb along her jaw. "Convinced yet?"

She blinked a few times, and that sweet, sensual haze in her eyes cleared, which was quickly replaced with a stubborn resolution. "No," she replied as the hands still splayed on my chest gave a firm push.

I instantly released her and stepped back, not because I was deterred or giving up, not when that seductive kiss had just told me everything I needed to know. For the moment, I was granting her the necessary space to process what had just happened, but I wasn't done with her. Not even close. That kiss was just the beginning.

"If that hot, mutually satisfying kiss didn't persuade you to change your mind, then I guess I need to step up my game," I teased, though I was one hundred percent serious about pursuing her. "I'll see you later, sweetheart."

I headed for the front of the studio and walked out the door without looking back.

Game on.

CHAPTER 3

Kendall

"*I* can see why you come so highly recommended. You captured the exact tone I wanted for these erotic pictures, all without revealing our faces."

The awe in my client's voice made me smile. I was incredibly relieved that I'd managed to give Stacie the kind of seductive images she'd requested, especially considering the strict guidelines the other woman had given me for the photo shoot. "I'm glad you're happy with the final photos."

"Oh, I am. Very much so. And Richard is going to love them, too." Stacie glanced from the portfolio on my laptop showcasing all the edited photos I'd taken a week ago, and met my gaze. "He was nervous about doing the couple's session and would only agree if the poses didn't show our facial features. I have to confess that I wasn't sure I'd like the end results, but these shots are just phenomenal and have exceeded my expectations."

Their couple's session had been definitely unique and different from any other boudoir session I had ever done before, but I'd embraced the challenge and enjoyed working with them as a couple, which was a side of my business I was trying to grow. The day of the photo shoot, Stacie had introduced the gentleman she'd brought with her as just "Richard." No last name, not that it was necessary. He was clearly older than Stacie but still classically handsome, with short dark hair and chiseled features. He'd been dressed in an expensive-looking charcoal-gray business suit.

I had had no idea what their relationship was, but within a half hour into their session, it had become evident that the two were intimate and that Stacie liked having the upper hand in sexual situations. As the layers of clothes were shed down to briefs and barely there lingerie, so were their inhibitions—with the only requirement that I not reveal their faces in any way. In nearly nude shots, I'd posed them strategically, using Stacie's long, wavy, strawberry-blonde hair to cover their faces. A tip of their heads removed their features from the shot, and the placement of their bodies and limbs also helped to conceal their identities.

I spent another forty minutes with Stacie, noting the selection of photos the other woman wanted, which was nearly all of them. Without batting an eye at the price, Stacie chose the Pure Bliss Platinum Package that also included a red leather-bound photo book of all the provocative photographs, to use as an intimate keepsake.

Once the appointment was over and it was quiet in the studio, I pulled up the collection of photographs I'd taken of Jase and Nicole. The author had selected five of the shots for her book cover and other promotional items, and now all I had to do was edit the pictures to the client's liking. I managed to get through the first four photos in a semi-detached manner, but it was the last image of Jase at his most dominant that ignited a liquid kind of heat in my veins.

Jase did aggressive and domineering extremely well, in a way that looked instinctive and natural. The effortless way he restrained Nicole's hands over her head, the strain of muscle bisecting his back as he kept her pinned beneath him, and the strong flex of his hips against hers were so erotic it made me feel breathless. Everything about him exuded power and control, along with the promise of hot sex, and I found myself clenching my thighs in response to the pulsing need settling between.

I groaned and bit my bottom lip. This was the photo that had elicited a dozen naughty, depraved fantasies over the course of the past two nights since I'd last seen Jase. The searing kiss he'd stolen before walking out of my studio had fueled the fire deep inside my belly, made me simmer and burn and ache for more than just the impersonal hum of a silicone vibrator to take the edge off my growing desire. The sensual memory of his mouth consuming mine kept reminding me how much time had passed since I'd felt the touch of a real man. Jase had started the craving, and now I was at a loss as to how to make it go away, damn him.

The buzz of my phone on the desk startled me back to the present. I unlocked the screen and read the text message from Stephanie: *Found those black sheer drapes you wanted for the studio bedroom. I'll bring them with me to our get-together tonight at Paige's. See you in about an hour!*

"Crap," I muttered. I'd forgotten all about our girls' night out.

Getting back to work, I finished editing the last photo, then sent them all off to the author. After backing up my files, I put the external drive in my small office safe, then shut down my computer to take home with me, as I did every night. I cleaned off my desk, flipped quickly through my stack of mail to make sure there wasn't anything important I needed to take care of, and came to a stop when I saw a pristine white envelope addressed to me.

There was no return address. Nothing to indicate where or who the piece of mail had come from. Frowning, I opened the flap and removed the heavy card stock tucked inside. My heart raced as I read the word *Welcome* embossed in black across the front, then below that, an invitation to The Players Club, a private, members-only sex club in Fallbrook.

Excitement and nerves swirled in my stomach at the thought of using the invitation in my hand. I read the details once more. *Your presence is requested at the annual fund-raising silent charity auction, A Night of Pleasure, where you will be auctioned off as a plaything to one lucky bidder.* The date was this Saturday, at eight p.m.

Oh, wow. I wasn't sure how I felt about the auction and being bid on by a stranger—apprehensive, aroused, and thrilled were all applicable emotions—but I was curious enough about getting a peek inside the exclusive Players Club and all its debauchery to consider going. *Maybe.*

First, I needed to find out who had sent me the invitation. It had to have been either Jillian, Raina, or Paige, since the three of them had already been there and had access to the club's amenities through the men in their lives. And since I was seeing them tonight at our get-together, one of them was going to have to fess up.

* * *

I TOOK a drink of the peach mojito that Paige had made for everyone, while glancing over the rim at the three women sitting on the couch across from me: Paige, Jillian, and Raina. Stephanie and Summer sat in chairs on either side of me, the six of us making a tight-knit circle in Paige's living room.

The last piece of gossip had died down, as had the laughter and ribald comments when Summer had told us about a prominent councilman coming into Couture Corsets to supposedly buy a corset for his wife, except he'd gone into the dressing room to try it on himself. The rumors that the older man liked to cross-dress were apparently true.

Swallowing the sweet taste of crushed peaches and smooth rum, I set my glass on the table next to my chair and eyed the women on the sofa. "So, which one of you mailed me an invitation to The Players Club?"

The three women looked at one another, an

array of confusion, surprise, and bemusement flitting across their faces as each one waited for the other to speak up.

Jillian was the first to respond. "I didn't do it."

Paige shook her head. "Neither did I."

Everyone glanced at Raina expectantly, but she held her hands up in denial, too. "Me, either."

I had a hard time believing any of them, considering how they'd each come to receive their own invitations to the club—from each other.

"Well, Stephanie and I certainly don't have access to the club," Summer said as she refilled her glass from the pitcher of peach mojito sitting on the coffee table. "So, if the three of you didn't do it, who did?" she asked, genuinely confused.

"Oooh, I love a good mystery." Stephanie sat forward, her tone intrigued.

"Maybe someone here *wanted* it to remain a mystery," Raina suggested. "And that's why the invitation was mailed instead of presented in person."

"But who, and why?" I persisted.

"Who cares who or why?" Paige said, dismissing those details as inconsequential. "I'm more interested in knowing if you're going to go."

"Me, too," Summer chimed in, and grinned at me. "And if your answer is no, you can just pass along the invitation to me."

"You are *so* going," Stephanie said, a sudden wicked gleam in her eyes. "Remember that conversation we had about Grant the chiropractor the other day?"

"How can I forget?" I teased sarcastically. My friend had given me a whole lot to think about—attraction, desire, sparks. None of which I'd felt with Grant. And everything I'd experienced, and more, with just one kiss from Jase. A kiss that made me hot and restless just *thinking* about it.

Stephanie finished off her cocktail and kept going. "Well, before you decide to get all serious with Mr. Serious, I think you need to at least experience one night of scorching hot, no-holds-barred sex with some divine male creature whose sole purpose is to worship your body and grant you as many orgasms as your heart can handle."

I laughed. "You are so outrageous." But damn if that didn't sound . . . deviously naughty, and fun. *A Night of Pleasure*, as my invitation had stated. One evening, auctioned off to a stranger. No names exchanged. Just wild, anonymous, anything-goes sex to end my two-year drought before I settled down with someone dependable and stable. It was my golden opportunity to experience the kind of passion and lust I'd only fantasized about, and maybe, hopefully, a night of abandon would also finally get Jase Burns out of my head so I could focus better on the feelings I might be able to develop for Grant.

A slow, exhilarating sensation slid through me. I'd let my friends play their games. It really didn't matter which one of these women had sent me the invitation. I'd just accept the gift for what it was and be open to all the possibilities. I'd throw my normal reservations away and *go for it*.

With that thought in mind, I lifted my glass for a toast. "I'm doing it. I'm going to The Players Club," I announced, which earned me big smiles of approval from the other women. "Here's to a night of pleasure."

Six glasses clinked together as Jillian added cheerfully, "To finding a man who will rock your world and leave you utterly, wonderfully exhausted and satisfied."

"To being bold and brazen and very, very bad," Raina said, waggling her brows playfully.

"And of course, to as many orgasms as you can handle!" Stephanie shouted above all the laughter, and all six of us let out a loud, raucous, and agreeable, "Cheers to that!"

CHAPTER 4

Kendall

I arrived at The Players Club forty minutes before the silent charity auction was scheduled to begin in order to attend the mandatory first-timers' orientation for anyone who'd never been up for bid before. *Yeah, that would be me—both a club and auction virgin,* I thought wryly as I listened to the activities coordinator give the men and women in the room an overview of the process and what to expect once the silent auction began and after it ended.

The exclusive establishment was all about safety, uncompromising rules and standards, and consensual encounters, with a universal safe word everyone was required to immediately heed if any situation became too uncomfortable or intense. Their strict policies were put in place to protect members and to assure that even though someone was the highest bidder, if there were any doubts or reluctance about being with the winner intimately, the participant had the right to decline the offer, which put my mind at ease.

I really had no idea what to expect once I was matched up with my bidder. While I was open to stepping outside my very square box and exploring other things for one night, I appreciated the safeguard of knowing I could say *red* at any time, and my request to stop any activity would be respected.

I filled out a form on my personal hard and soft limits, which would then be uploaded to the silent auction bidding app under my profile. That way, the bidder would know up front what type of play I was and wasn't comfortable with. Blood play, electro play, humiliation, and anything hard-core, *absolutely not*. Voyeurism, fantasy rooms, *maybe*. Spanking, domination, restraints, hair pulling...*oh, yes, please*, my inner hussy agreed enthusiastically.

I bit my bottom lip as I recalled the way my body had pulsed with desire when Jase had tugged on my hair while kissing me, and how much I'd liked that light sting of pain, if my hardening nipples were any indication. I quickly shook my head of that thought and checked the "no limit" box for those particular items. I was here to forget about Jase, not compare his sexual expertise with other men.

Finished with the seemingly endless list—who knew there were so many fetishes and kinks to consider?—I handed the form to the coordinator, who then gave me a pin to wear with a number that matched my profile on the app. No names were exchanged with bidders unless I wanted to supply that information, and since tonight's fling was a one-time deal, I preferred the security of anonymity.

Once everyone was done with the paperwork, we were escorted into a beautifully decorated ballroom, where other men and women were already waiting for the evening's eligible playthings to arrive for the silent auction. Impeccably dressed waitstaff walked through the room with trays of champagne and appetizers, and a bar area was set up for those who wanted a mixed cocktail, though a two-drink maximum applied, even here at the auction.

Let the mingling begin.

After picking up a fluted glass of champagne from a passing waiter, I took a fortifying drink of the sparkling wine. I attempted to shake off my nerves as a good-looking man started walking toward me, his stride purposeful and his gaze appreciative as he took in the sexy black dress I'd worn that hugged my curves and was designed with a neckline that came together in a very deep vee in the front. The cut was so low there was no way to wear a bra. Not that I needed one with my small, firm, size-B breasts.

He stopped in front of me. Up close, he appeared to be in his late thirties, and very comfortable in this setting. His gaze quickly dropped to the pin on my dress, then rose back up to my face.

"So, Ms. Number Nine," he said with a

charming smile that instantly put me at ease. "How are you doing tonight?"

I returned his smile. "Very well, and you?"

"My evening just got immensely better." His tawny eyes gleamed playfully, his demeanor conveying a fun, easygoing vibe. "My name is Wyatt. What made you decide to offer yourself up for bid tonight?"

"Charity?" I joked lightly. No way was I about to tell him that I was here to end a two-year dry spell.

He chuckled. "Yes, of course, it's all about *charity*," he agreed humorously. "But is there something specific you're looking for tonight at The Players Club? Anything in particular you'd like to indulge in that you've never tried before?"

Clearly, he was a seasoned regular at the club. Which suddenly made me feel way out of my league. "This is my first time here, so I'm not quite sure what I want to indulge in," I confessed, wanting to make sure Wyatt was well aware of my own *lack* of experience in a sex club atmosphere. "I guess I'm open to suggestions, as long as we stay within my limits."

He lifted the cell phone in his hand and used his thumb to scroll through the bidding app, then pulled up my profile based on the number nine on my pin. He quickly read my limit list while I finished off my champagne.

"Hmm," he contemplated as he glanced back at me, definite interest brightening his gaze. "I do enjoy breaking in a newcomer. I think the two of us could have a lot of fun together."

Wyatt was attractive enough and seemed like a good match. He wasn't overbearing and appeared willing to stay within my comfort zone. I just wished I felt something more with him—some kind of spark, butterflies, or even sexual tension. Then again, maybe I was over-analyzing the situation and my expectations about tonight were way too high.

"Excuse me," another man said as he gently grabbed my arm while sending a competitive look in Wyatt's direction. "I'm going to steal this stunningly gorgeous woman away from you."

Wyatt raised a brow in friendly rivalry. "Don't get too attached, Dawson. I already put in a bid for her, so she's going to be mine."

"Cocky bastard," Dawson replied jokingly,

and Wyatt laughed. "She's not yours unless you're the highest bidder at the end of the hour, which I plan to be."

"Yeah, good luck with that, buddy." Wyatt winked confidently at me. "I'll see you real soon, Number Nine."

"Looks like there's going to be a fierce bidding war over you tonight," Dawson mused, his smile warm and friendly, his tone jovial. "Wouldn't be the first time Wyatt and I fought over a woman here at the club. Unless you wouldn't mind being shared?"

I quickly shook my head to dispel any notion he had of a threesome. "Absolutely not. That's a hard limit for me. I'm strictly a one-man kind of woman."

"Noted," Dawson said with a quirk of his lips. "Can't blame a man for asking—and hoping."

Picking up my hand, he tucked it into the crook of his arm and led me to a quiet sitting area, where we spent the next few minutes talking until another gentleman interrupted us and drew me away from Dawson to get to know me better.

The next hour passed much quicker than I

would have thought. I felt as though I were at a speed-dating event more than an auction at a sex club, but when the auctioneer announced that it was time to match up the highest bidders with the person they'd won, I was reminded of what I was *really* here for. In a matter of minutes, some man would claim me as his plaything for the night, and I figured it was a toss-up between Wyatt and Dawson.

Couples were paired off, and when my number was called to stand on the platform for my winner to claim, I was instead approached by one of the event's hostesses. "Your winning bidder requested that I escort you to a private room he reserved for the two of you. If you'll follow me, I'll take you there."

"Okay." Despite my sudden bout of nerves, I fell into step behind the younger woman, who led me through the club to a more secluded wing of the mansion.

We passed different-colored doors in vibrant, jewel-toned shades—ruby red, amethyst purple, emerald green—until the hostess stopped at the panel painted a sapphire blue. She inserted a code into the digital keypad on the wall, and the door unlocked with a soft click.

The other woman stepped aside and smiled. "Here you go. Enjoy your evening."

"Thank you," I said and waited until the hostess walked away and I was alone in the hallway.

I had no idea what to expect, and with my heart suddenly beating hard and fast in my chest, I stepped over the threshold before I lost the courage to do so. Once I was inside, I closed the door, and the sound of the lock clicking into place echoed in the silent room.

It took my eyes a few seconds to adjust to the softer, subtler lighting. A glittering crystal chandelier overhead produced just enough illumination to set the scene for seduction. At least a dozen tapered candles flickered from a table near the luxurious four-poster bed, which was covered in silky blue linens. The elegantly carved canopy and headboard were inlaid with mirrors, and to my right was a play area set up with odd-shaped pieces of furniture covered in leather, along with strange contraptions hanging from the walls and ceilings, and shelves of other devices and implements for more elevated sex play.

I shivered as I caught sight of an entire rack of assorted floggers, canes, and crops. *What the hell have I gotten myself into? And with whom?*

Just as the thought passed through my mind, a soft sound came from across the room, and my gaze immediately searched the shadowed corner. I could just barely make out the outline of a male form sitting in a chair, and when he stood up and started toward me, my breath caught in my throat as I watched *Jase* gradually close the distance between us.

Shock rendered me speechless, and all I could do was take in his bare feet, the black slacks that fit him to perfection, and the fact that he'd already stripped out of his shirt—as if he'd made himself comfortable while waiting for me to arrive. His chest was bare, and each step he took made the toned muscles along his abdomen flex and my own stomach clench.

He stopped an arm's length away from me, and I jerked my gaze to his gorgeous face, watching as a slow smile kicked up the corners of his sensual mouth.

"Hello, sweetheart," he greeted me.

Just the intimate sound of his voice, and the way his eyes trailed over me, made my insides liquefy. The spark and heated chemistry that had been missing with Dawson and Wyatt roared to life now. The sexual tension between me and Jase was already so palpable, and he hadn't even touched me.

I swallowed hard, my mind racing with so many questions. Jase hadn't been a participant at the auction, so why was I there with *him*? "What are *you* doing here?"

He raised a light brown brow, as if the answer was obvious. "I submitted the winning bid, which means you're all mine for tonight, to do with as I please. Within your limits, of course," he added softly.

You're all mine for tonight, to do with as I please. Even as his statement caused delicious tremors to take hold, I shook my head in confusion, trying to make sense of it all. "But...*how?*"

"It's a silent auction, and with the app, you can pretty much bid from anywhere," he explained easily. "Though I do have to say, I was damn lucky to come in as the highest bid when the auction ended, considering the three-way bidding war between myself, Dawson, and Wyatt. It was damn close."

I didn't even want to know how high that final, winning offer had been, and the price Jase had paid to secure a night with me. I still couldn't believe he was here, that he'd known about the auction, about me being up for bid . . . and then realization struck. *Oh, my God.* "*You* sent me the invitation to The Players Club to participate in tonight's charity auction." It wasn't a question, but now it made sense that my girlfriends had denied knowing anything about the invite. "Why?"

"You know exactly *why*, Kendall." His eyes were dark and serious, so seductive and hypnotic. "I'm stepping up my game just like I told you I would, and doing whatever it takes to convince you to give me a chance. Though I find it incredibly interesting that you won't go out on a date with me, yet you accepted an invitation to The Players Club to hook up with a potential stranger."

I winced in embarrassment, unable to believe he was calling me out on those two contrasting principles, but I couldn't bring myself to argue his point out loud when my explanation was much too revealing. With a stranger, I didn't have to worry about a connection or expectations or anything complicated. It was just *sex*, and I could walk away without any emotional attachments.

But dating Jase... I already knew that the intense attraction between us had the potential to make things far more tangled and involved, and I was trying to protect both of us by turning him down. With someone as young as him, when we were at different points in our lives—me looking to settle down and him just a few years out of the military and figuring out his own life—well, it was a recipe for the kind of pain and disaster my ex-husband had already put me through.

When I remained quiet, he reached out and brazenly traced the deep opening in the front of my dress, his fingertips deliberately brushing along the swell of my breasts. I bit my bottom lip as my nipples beaded tight and hard against the material, and he did nothing to hide his satisfaction as he raised his gaze back to mine.

"So, I guess the question is, are you going to leave because you're afraid you might enjoy yourself too much, or will you stay and give me the very expensive evening I rightfully won, and claim the *night of pleasure* that you came to The Players Club for?"

"You don't play fair." My body ached for what he was offering, what I'd been without for two long years. The sultry slide of eager male hands on my skin. The decadent feel of a man's mouth sucking my breasts, his tongue delving between my thighs.

A hot, desperate shiver stole through me. I was torn. Conflicted. My body's desires waged war with my logical mind, and all the reasons this was a very bad idea were being overruled by my own selfish needs. I couldn't remember the last time, if ever, that a man had made me feel so wanted. So desired. So filled with anticipation.

"The way I see it, it's a win-win situation for both of us. Pleasure for pleasure," Jase said as he circled around to stand behind me, but not before I caught a glimpse of something more intimate in his eyes. Something that told me he wanted a whole lot more than just one simple night of pleasure from me.

Firmly gripping my hips in his hands, he

drew me a step back, until our bodies aligned and I could feel his hard, thick, substantial erection pressing insistently against my bottom. I closed my eyes as a rush of moisture dampened my panties and my sex pulsed. I swallowed back a groan, struggling against the shameless urge to bend over, spread my legs, and beg him to fill me, *take me*.

"I want you so fucking bad," he said gruffly, his warm breath feathering against the side of my neck. "The choice to stay or go is ultimately up to you. But if you do stay, I'm letting you know right up front that I'm going to be in control of *everything* that happens tonight. You'll be mine in every sense of the word."

The heated promise, the demand in his voice obliterated the last of my resistance. I'd come to The Players Club for sex and sin. To be bold and daring and walk away physically satisfied. I'd be crazy not to experience it all with a man who made me burn hot with lust with just a look.

Lust. Yes, that's all this was. All it could be. I'd give myself, and Jase, this one night to get this crazy attraction out of our system, then I'd walk away before he did it first. Because eventually, I knew he would.

"I'll...I'll stay." *No backing out now.*

"Good answer," he said, his tone undeniably pleased as he stepped back and let his clenched fingers drop from my hips—but just long enough to raise his hands to the zipper securing my dress. "First things first. I want this dress off."

He lowered the metal tab, inch by inch, all the way to the base of my spine. He pushed the sleeves off my arms, and the silky material slid down my body on its own and pooled around my feet, leaving me in just a pair of lacy, sheer black panties. I stepped out of the dress, then bent to take off my strappy high heels.

"Leave them on," he said, the brusque tone of his voice startling me.

I straightened, and before I could turn around to face him, he came up behind me again. This time when he pulled me back against him, it was all skin-on-skin contact. The heat of his chest along my spine and the firm press of his flattened palms gliding up my abdomen felt heavenly, the strength of his touch both arousing and relaxing me so that I leaned more fully into him.

If I were a cat, I would have rubbed shamelessly against him and purred.

His hands reached my breasts, cupping them, molding them, squeezing them until my nipples were tight and hard and aching. "Look around," he said as he plucked and rolled those sensitive peaks between his fingers in such a wicked way I felt the pull all the way down between my legs. "Is there anything in this room that you're curious about or that you'd like to try? Tell me what you want, and I'll make it happen."

Another pinch of his fingers and my knees nearly buckled. I pressed my hands back against his thighs and gripped the fabric of his slacks in my fists so I had something, anything, to hold on to while he continued to tease my breasts. My half-lidded gaze slid across the room to the St. Andrew's Cross, then the sex swing, and finally the spanking bench. I felt completely out of my element.

"I've never done anything like this before," I admitted and, in that moment, wished I was more experienced. More worldly, instead of so vanilla. But conventional sex was all I knew and was the sum of my ten-year marriage.

His hands fell away from my breasts. Turning me around, he maneuvered me backwards a few steps until I was pressed up against the nearest wall. He splayed his palms on either side of my shoulders, his gaze so heated and hungry, his demeanor so dominating it took my breath away and sent a secret thrill spiraling through me.

"It's all about what feels good and turns you on," he murmured as he skimmed his fingers along my collarbone, slowly trailed them down my chest, and lightly circled around my areole.

God, his touch alone felt good and turned me on. My nipples were puckered so tight they hurt, and arousal thickened inside me. "I don't know what I want," I said, which was the truth. At this moment, my thoughts were much too scattered to process everything this room had to offer. "It's all so overwhelming." *He* was overwhelming.

He lowered his head and nuzzled his warm lips against my throat. "Then let me help you figure it out," he said as he slid his hand down my torso and directly into my panties.

With his knee, he nudged my legs farther apart to make more room for his hand to move between my thighs, for his long, talented fingers to stroke along my sex and drive me mindless with need. My head fell back against the wall, and I released a strangled moan as my hips rocked shamelessly against his deliciously wicked touch.

His teeth scraped across my neck and up to my ear. "Tell me, when you're lying in bed at night and you're touching yourself like this, what do you think about to get your pussy hot and wet?" He caught my sensitive clit between his index and middle fingers and gave it a gentle tug that made me jolt and gasp. "What deep, dark fantasies do you spin in your mind that makes you come long and hard and scream from the sheer force of your orgasm?"

I was panting for breath, my body on edge and clamoring for the release Jase held just out of my reach. And now he wanted me to spill those forbidden secrets I'd never shared with anyone else. I swallowed hard, unsure I could verbalize something so incredibly personal and intimate. "Jase…please."

He lifted his head and stared at my face, his

jaw clenched tight. The unrelenting determination in his expression made my heart race, showing me a different side to the flirtatious male model who'd been nothing but charming and playful in my studio. This man in front of me was in control. Sexually assertive. And shockingly intense.

And everything within me responded to that authority in a way I never would have expected.

He sank his free hand into my hair and wrapped the strands around his wrist to keep my head turned up toward his. "If you want to come, tell me those fantasies," he demanded while his skilled fingers caressed my clit with precise, circling strokes. "And I don't want the sweet, sugar-coated version. I want to know every *filthy* detail."

CHAPTER 5

Kendall

y legs went weak, from Jase's unfiltered words and the way he kept me right on the razor-sharp edge of climaxing. I knew what I had to do to end this madness, and what had I come to The Players Club for if not to be adventurous and fearless when it came to sex? Jase wasn't a stranger but someone I trusted and felt safe with. There was no doubt in my mind that if I so much as uttered the safe word, any scenario would immediately end.

But stopping this provocative seduction wasn't what I wanted. Not when I was just getting a small taste of the kind of ecstasy I'd only imagined.

He was watching me so avidly, waiting for me to reveal *every filthy detail*, and I gave him what he wanted. "I think about...being taken from behind while I'm pinned down and tied up."

He arched a taunting brow as if to say, *that's all you got?* "Surely you can do better than that, sweetheart."

I ignored the way my skin flushed at the mocking tone of his voice, the way my body trembled with each swipe of his fingers along my sex. "While I'm restrained and helpless...I want to be fucked, hard and deep and rough." The confession poured out of me in a rush.

The grin that curved his lips was pure sin. "That's exactly how I like to fuck. Hard. Aggressive. And dirty. Tonight, we're going to make your fantasy happen."

Sensation flooded my extremities in a hot, wet rush. The swelling, the moisture gathering, my shallow exhale—the lust glowing in his eyes told me he felt it all.

"You are so fucking ready for this," he rasped darkly.

I wasn't sure if he was referring to the fantasy or the orgasm, but I wanted both. "Yes, please," I begged huskily.

His lips came crashing down on mine, his chest crushing against my bare breasts as he pinned me against the wall with his rock-hard body. His mouth devoured, his tongue claimed, and when he pushed two long fingers deep inside me, I went shamelessly wild. No longer held back by any mental restraints, I twisted against him to get closer and used my hands to grip the muscles along his back. He lured me with another hot sweep of his tongue inside my mouth, another thrust of his fingers. I whimpered desperately against his lips and sank my nails into his skin.

Without thinking, I raised my right knee and wrapped my leg high around his hip, opening myself completely to him. He let out a ragged hiss of breath and pushed his hand harder between my thighs, rubbed his thumb firm and fast against my clitoris, and I finally splintered apart. Passion and pleasure collided in a combustible combination unlike anything

I'd ever experienced before, searing me from the inside out.

With a deep-throated growl, Jase jerked his head back, tearing his mouth from mine so he could witness me unraveling. His dark, heavy-lidded gaze took it all in, watching my changing expression...watching as I arched my neck and my lower body strained against his as I rode his hand...watching as my lips parted and I screamed so loud my throat felt raw.

Completely, utterly spent, I collapsed against Jase. I clung to him as my entire body shook with the aftershocks, fearful that my legs would give out on me at any second. As if knowing how weak I was after that monstrous orgasm, he circled an arm around my waist, holding me close to his chest while I tried to recover. He tucked my head against his neck, and the hand still in my hair gently massaged my scalp. He was so big, so strong, and he smelled so good I let myself snuggle against him.

The adrenaline rush subsided, my heart rate calmed, and I suddenly became aware of the rigid length of his erection pressing insistently against my stomach. But he made no move to remove his pants and take this encounter to its logical conclusion. He'd given me an earth-shattering orgasm, I was way more than willing to return the favor…yet he wasn't in a big hurry to get himself off.

Wow. What a novelty.

Another quiet minute passed before he gently tipped my head back so he could look into my eyes, which I was sure were completely dazed. He searched my face, the affection in his gaze startling me. "You okay?"

There was nothing smug or satisfied about his tone—when he had every right to be a little cocky after that seduction and my acquiescence. Instead, the genuine concern and care in his voice touched me in places that had no business being a part of tonight's fling.

I nodded and smiled. "Yeah, I think so."

Now the arrogant grin appeared, and I had to admit it was sexy as hell. "That was hotter than fuck."

I laughed a little self-consciously when I thought about how uninhibited I'd just been, and how good it felt. "*That* was the result of two years of pent-up lust." Too late, I realized just how much I'd revealed.

A disbelieving frown slanted his brows. "Is that seriously how long it's been since you've been with a man?"

There was no sense in lying. "Yes. Since my divorce."

He appeared honestly shocked. "Damn. You've got a lot of making up to do."

I was grateful that he'd opted for humor instead of making it an issue. "That orgasm was definitely a great start." Feeling much too comfortable in his arms, I gently pushed away, and he let me go.

"There's a whole lot more where that came from." He waggled his brows, looking young and boyishly playful. Cute, even.

Nope, don't go there, girl, not tonight.

"Can you walk over to the bed on your own?" he asked.

My legs were still a bit wobbly but much steadier now. "I'm good."

I made it over to the big bed and stood by the side, watching as he strolled over to the rack of toys and restraints hanging on the wall. He joined me after selecting wrist cuffs with metal hardware attached, and tossed them to the far side of the bed.

Oh, God, this was really going to happen.

He met my gaze for a moment. "If any of what's about to happen gets too intense for you, just use the safe word and it ends."

I acknowledged him with a nod.

He shifted on his feet, and along with that came a compelling switch in his expression, his entire disposition. His eyes challenged me, drew me in, dark and hot. "Are you ready for a hard, dirty fuck?"

A delicious shiver coursed through me. "Yes," I whispered.

"Lie down on your back on the bed," he instructed.

Still wearing just my panties and heels, I slid across the mattress and assumed the position he requested, my gaze riveted to my reflection in the mirror inlaid in the overhead canopy. My blonde hair was disheveled from his hands, my lips pink and swollen from his mouth, and my skin was flushed with an infusion of desire and anticipation. Had I ever in my life looked so debauched? No, *never*, but I liked what I saw in the mirror—a sexy, sensual woman who wasn't holding back tonight.

Jase moved up onto the bed after me and

straddled my waist. His hard, muscular thighs pressed tightly against my sides, the weight of his body leaving me no way to escape. His hungry gaze leisurely traveled from my full, aching breasts to my face, and there was no way I could miss the thick length of his erection straining against the front of his slacks.

"Put your hands above your head," he ordered.

I did as he asked, and he reached for the restraints he'd put on the bed. Leaning over me, he looped the silver chain connecting the leather cuffs through the wooden slat in the headboard to keep my arms straight, and buckled my wrists into each soft, fur-lined cuff. I tried to move my arms, but there was no slack at all. I swallowed hard just as he braced his hands on either side of my head, his features dark and a little dangerous.

"I like you like this," he said huskily. "Naked and spread out for me. Under my control. *Mine.*"

The last word came out on a possessive growl as he lowered his mouth to mine and kissed me. Hard. Deep. Thoroughly. Drugging my mind and making my body burn again in no time flat. When he had his fill of my mouth, he dragged his damp lips along the side of my neck, deliberately scraping his teeth across my tender skin as he slid down my body, until he was able to take my breast into his mouth.

I moaned as he sucked hard and deep on the stiff, sensitive tip. He alternated between stinging bites of pain on my nipple and the soothing swirl of his tongue, then repeated the process on my other breast until I was panting impatiently. He trailed more hot, wet, torturous kisses down my quivering belly, dipped his wicked tongue into my navel, and licked a searing path straight down to the waistband of my panties.

Need shot straight to my core, and I tried to move my hips to push up against Jase, but he didn't budge. He still sat astride my body, his strong thighs like steel bands against the sides of my legs as he continued his downward quest.

He nuzzled his nose against my mound, his exhale of breath scorching hot against my inner thigh. "I can smell how fucking wet and aroused you are," he rasped right before he flicked his tongue down the front panel of my damp panties and traced my slit through the drenched silk, bringing me right back up to a fevered pitch, where another blistering orgasm was only a stroke away.

I cried out, pulling on my restraints as my back arched off the bed and my hips bucked against his mouth. Beyond desperate, beyond shame, I was willing to do or say anything if he would just let me spread my legs for him so I could feel the full effect of his tongue on me. "Oh, God, Jase, *please*."

He finally sat up, his lower body now straddling my legs down by my knees. I stared up at him, watching the clench of his jaw, seeing the lust and need etched across his features as he unbuckled his belt and pulled the strip of leather through the loops. I waited for him to remove his pants, which would give me room to open my legs, but instead he took his belt and wrapped it around my thighs, then secured the strap above my knees, making me realize just how helpless I actually was.

My heart slammed against my chest, and I drew in a shaky breath, suddenly feeling defenseless and vulnerable. This wasn't at all what I'd expected, yet when Jase remained still,

I realized he was waiting for my racing pulse to calm, to accept that I was actually the one with all the power and could stop him at any time.

When I said nothing, he moved off me and then the bed. I panicked as he walked away, wondering if *he* intended to end the scene, and that thought was enough to make me realize just how badly I wanted this with him. "Jase..."

"Don't worry, sweetheart," he murmured softly. "I'm not going far, and we're not done. I'll be right back."

I watched him head across the room and retrieve something from a dresser drawer. When he returned, he tossed a few foil packages on the mattress beside me, along with a small vibrator toy in its original packaging. My eyes widened at the latter, and with a wicked grin, he grabbed my hips and flipped me over so I was now on my stomach—still stretched out and bound and his for the taking, however he wanted.

He removed his pants, giving me only a quick second to appreciate how sculpted his entire body was, including the immense length of his cock, before he came up behind me on the bed. Securing a muscled arm around my midsection, he elevated my lower body so that I was on my knees and my bottom positioned high in the air. The pull of the cuffs around my wrists straightened my arms and forced my upper body to rest flat on the mattress.

Grabbing the waistband of the black lace underwear I still wore, he slid them off of me. They could only go as far as the belt around my legs, and in my mind I could imagine how naughty and indecent that made me look, with my panties bunched around my thighs and nothing else but the black heels on my feet. I *felt* naughty, and very, very turned on.

"Jesus, you have a great ass," he said appreciatively as he ran a warm hand over the curve of my backside, then smacked me with a flattened palm.

I gasped and jerked at the unexpected and firm swat, but there was nowhere to go as the shocking burn gradually gave way to a pleasant heat that made my sex throb with a renewed ache. His hand pushed between my bound thighs, his fingers stroking along my slick flesh, then caressing the hard little nub of my clit before he thrust two long fingers deep inside my body. I moaned, my hips moving in rhythm to his touch as he repeated the process, over and over, faster and faster—*stroke, caress, thrust*—building an avalanche of sensation between my thighs that superseded anything I'd ever experienced before.

He worked me into a fevered pitch of need, and through the lust clouding my mind, I knew that was exactly his intent—to make me wild again, make me desperate for him. *To make me his.*

The emotional impact of that realization shuddered through me, even as another fierce orgasm peaked within. Right as I was on the brink of falling over, his touch was gone.

I whimpered at the loss, then heard the crinkling sound of a foil package being torn open as he took care of protection. Whatever was in the tiny box was also removed, and then he was back. Bracing his thighs along the outsides of mine, he held my hip steady with one hand and used his other to slide the head of his cock between my thighs and through my drenched pussy. Positioning the tip against my entrance, he pushed just a few inches inside, teasing me with what I ached for so badly.

"Are you ready for this?" he demanded as

his hand connected against my ass again, which caused my body to clench around his shaft. "To get fucked so hard that you'll be sore for the next week?"

"Yes," I said, much too anxiously.

"Say it, Kendall." His voice was dark, commanding, and that, too, sent a secret thrill rushing through me.

"Fuck me, Jase." The dirty words fell from my lips freely.

With a low, feral growl, he slammed into me, so hard and deep I cried out at the relentless force of his driving thrust, at the thick length filling me so full I couldn't breathe. He pushed my hips down and stretched his body along the length of mine until he was positioned over me, behind me, his solid weight keeping me enslaved beneath him. Wrapping a strong hand around my throat, he used it to tip my head back so that his lips could skim my cheek, his damp, erratic breath heating my skin as he pumped his cock in and out of me.

I couldn't move of my own accord, could only submit to the way he dominated my body, and I loved the illicit sensation, loved the erotic fantasy of being taken. I felt every inch of him as he moved, felt the heat and friction grow between my legs as he ground his hips against my ass and buried himself to the hilt, over and over.

He slid his free hand under my body and burrowed his middle finger into the folds of my sex. My mind only had a quick second to register a startling vibration—*and the fact that, oh, God, he was using a finger vibe*—before he aligned that pulsating device right against my sensitive clit.

Every nerve ending in my pussy jolted, as if he'd just touched me with a live wire. The searing, sensory assault was torment and ecstasy all rolled into the unbearable desire to climax again. I clawed at the sheets with my hands, dying to widen my legs, but all I could do was buck and thrash my hips against his and pant and moan with the maddening need for release.

His thrusts grew heavier, longer, his cock seemingly getting thicker, harder with each rough, jackhammer stroke. The fingers around my neck tightened as his entire body tensed over mine, his chest heaving against my back, his lips parted against my throat as he tunneled farther inside me, claiming me in such a primitive, unrefined way.

"*Oh, fuck*," he rasped, and with one last driving flex of his hips, he groaned and shuddered as he started to come.

The steady, insistent hum of the vibrator against my clit, combined with the throbbing hot pulse of Jase's cock surging inside me, stole the last of my sanity. My heartbeat roared in my ears as I shattered, disintegrated, and came apart so completely I knew I'd never be the same again. Swept up in such devastating pleasure, I vaguely heard him shout out his own release.

He withdrew his hand from between my legs, removing the relentless buzz of the toy so I could breathe normally again. Languid and exhausted, I sagged against the mattress. Behind me, Jase's body grew slack, as well, though he used his forearms to keep the heavy, muscled weight of his body from crushing me.

He placed soft, lazy kisses along my shoulder, and I couldn't stop the shiver that stole through me when his lips traveled up the side of my neck, nipping gently, until he reached my ear.

"So, was that hard and deep and rough enough for you?" he asked, a sexy, arrogant note in his voice as he reminded me of the erotic fantasy I'd shared with him.

A fantasy he'd fulfilled beyond my wildest expectations or anything I'd ever imagined, when even the man I'd been married to for ten years hadn't cared enough to discover what turned me on or be a little adventurous in the bedroom, which had left me feeling inadequate and lacking. And completely devastated when I'd discovered his affair with a barely legal nurse at the hospital where he'd been finishing his residency.

Yet in the span of an hour, Jase had somehow stripped me of my inhibitions and exposed those needs and desires I'd always kept hidden away. He'd made my body come alive again, had made me feel like a desirable, sexy woman for the first time in...forever. Possibly the first time *ever*.

The emotional impact of that realization overwhelmed me and made my chest tighten with the need to protect my heart and with the undeniable feelings Jase was beginning to awaken in me.

I swallowed hard and gave him the credit he deserved for making tonight very, very memorable. "That was perfect."

I could feel his content grin curve slowly against my neck. "*You're* perfect," he murmured huskily. "That was hotter and more intense than anything I've ever done or experienced before."

I heard the sincerity in his voice but refused to let it sway my emotions, which were already way too tangled up in what had just happened between us. "You belong to The Players Club," I said, striving for a wry tone to match the easygoing smile I tossed at him over my shoulder when I felt anything but playful. "I find it hard to believe that what we just did is the most erotic thing you've ever done with a woman."

He finally pulled out of me, and, still straddling my thighs from behind, he turned me over so I was on my back again—my arms and legs still completely bound. Leaning over me, he braced his hands on either side of my head, his dark coffee-colored gaze locked directly on mine. "It's not about the sex or the kink itself. It's all about the person you're with and how much they trust you with their body, and what you do with it. You, Kendall Shaw, gave your-self and your pleasure completely over to me, and *that* is what made what we just did so fucking satisfying."

I was coming to realize that I trusted him *too much*, and opening myself to another man that way again made me feel emotionally, inti-mately exposed. With each moment that passed with him staring down at me, my anxiety increased, because I knew that my attraction to Jase was more than just a physical thing, and that was the very last thing I wanted with him.

Overwhelmed by my unexpected feelings, *for him*, I needed space to breathe and think without him surrounding me. "I need you to release me," I said, more calmly than I felt inside.

He paused for a moment as if he was going to say something else but instead reached up and removed the restraints from my hands, then unbuckled the belt from my thighs before moving completely off of me to stand by the bed. I sat up and rubbed my wrists, my body already sore and tender from the deliciously aggressive way he'd used it.

"I'll be right back," he said reluctantly and

headed toward the adjoining bathroom, picking up his briefs and pants on the way.

He closed the door behind him, giving me the time alone I desperately needed without his intense gaze scrutinizing my face, which undoubtedly revealed way too much of the turmoil going on inside of me. I quickly pulled my panties back up, and, finding my dress on the floor, I slipped it on and zipped it as I debated leaving before he came back out of the bathroom.

I was so tempted to bolt. I had no experience with this kind of situation—a one-time hookup—and I dreaded the awkward post-sex conversation sure to come, which was so unnecessary. I'd gotten what I'd come to The Players Club for, and Jase had gotten exactly what he'd paid for. Our transaction was done.

My stomach clenched at the painful rationale when I knew what had just happened between me and Jase was so much more. The problem was, there couldn't be anything more between us, not when I was finally getting my life back on track after my divorce and needed to think about the future I wanted. A future that didn't include a man eight years younger than me. A hot, virile, gorgeous man who would eventually move on, once the heat and passion ebbed between us, to someone younger, sexier, and much closer to his own age.

I didn't think I could survive that kind of heartache all over again, and it was that excruciating thought that had me heading for the bedroom door to leave.

CHAPTER 6

Jase

I walked out of the bathroom just as Kendall reached the door. She stiffened when she heard me behind her and froze, one hand on the doorknob—caught in the act of fleeing.

I wasn't at all shocked to find her trying to sneak out of the room before I could stop her. Another few seconds and she would have accomplished her goal, but that wouldn't have prevented *me* from going after her.

"Leaving so soon?" I asked, trying to be casual, even though I recognized her attempted escape for what it was. She was literally running from what had just happened between us. Not the sex but the connection. The way her body had come alive for me. The way she'd given herself over to me. And how much she'd liked it.

She turned around, her chin lifting obstinately. "Yes, I'm leaving. We both got what we came here for."

So cut and dried. So impersonal it nearly gutted me. I managed, just barely, to tamp the frustration rising to the surface. "Is that what you think?" I asked, and strolled across the room toward her. "That I just wanted one night with you? That once I fucked you, it would be enough?"

She flinched at my words but held her ground. "It has to be enough. For both of us."

I stopped a few feet away, not wanting to crowd her or give her yet another reason to retreat when I wanted—no, *needed*—concrete answers. "Tell me, why does tonight have to be enough?"

Her own frustration flashed in her eyes. "I already told you why."

Yes, she had, that last day at her studio right before I'd kissed her. "You're divorced and you're eight years older than me," I reiterated, my jaw clenching impatiently. "Do you really think I give a shit about either?"

"You will, eventually," she shot back heatedly.

I couldn't believe that she honestly thought I'd use her for sex, then move on without a backwards glance. "You have that low of an opinion of me?"

"No, not you." She sighed and rubbed her fingers across her forehead. "I'm speaking from experience. My *personal* experience."

Ahhh, we were finally getting to the heart of the matter. Now I knew for certain that something had happened for her to put that guard up, and I wasn't about to let her leave until I understood those fears. Just like in the military, I couldn't deal with a threat until I knew exactly what kind of situation I was up against. The same principal applied with Kendall.

I moved around her and leaned against the closed door, clearly blocking her way out of the room until I had what I wanted. "Tell me about that personal experience."

"I'd rather not."

Her pink, swollen lips pursed oh-so-primly, and I had to resist the urge to throw her over my shoulder like a caveman, take her back to the bed, and tie her back down and seduce her until she spilled all her deep, dark secrets.

Instead, I crossed my arms over my chest and tried a more civil approach. "All I'm asking is that you make me understand what happened in the past to make you shut me out this way...before we ever get started. You owe me at least that much before you leave."

She folded her arms across her chest, as well, mimicking my determined stance and putting them at a stalemate. She met my gaze willfully, her stubborn expression making my palm itch to take her over my knee and spank her ass to let her know that I wouldn't tolerate her defiance.

Unfortunately, this wasn't a play session. Under the current circumstances, I was fairly certain Kendall wouldn't appreciate my more stimulating way of dealing with her insubordination.

So, instead, I raised a brow, silently communicating the fact that I had all night long and had no intentions of budging until I had answers.

As if she finally realized we were at an impasse, her tense shoulders dropped a fraction, the fight in her gradually subsiding. "Fine," she said softly.

Surprising me, she turned around and walked to the bed, then sat down on the edge of the mattress. She waved a hand toward a wooden-back chair normally used for discipline play. "Pull up a seat and make yourself comfortable," she said, her tone wry. "It's not a quick story."

Finally, I thought, relieved. Trying to lighten the moment, I flashed her a smile. "Luckily I bought you for the entire night." Positioning the chair right in front of her, I sat down.

The corner of her mouth twitched with amusement, then faded away before she spoke.

"I met my ex-husband, Drew, my junior year in college, when I was twenty-one, and we got married two years later. We were living in Los Angeles, and I got a job with an ad agency, while Drew, who intended to become a trauma surgeon, continued full time at UCLA School of Medicine."

I wasn't sure what this part of her past had to do with her resistance to date me, but I wanted to know everything about her, so I remained quiet and let her talk.

She ran her hands down the front of her thighs absently, smoothing the black fabric of her dress over her legs. "We lived in a tiny one-bedroom apartment, and I also did portrait photography on the side to make extra money to help pay off our school loans. And that's what I did for ten years while Drew continued his residency and internship. I wanted to start a family, but he was adamant that we wait and get all our loans paid off so we'd have no debt once he became a surgeon, and then we'd have kids. So, I worked my ass off. Between our two hectic schedules, we hardly had quality time together, but I just kept thinking about the end goal and being able to have a baby. I put in sixty-hour weeks at the advertising firm and worked weekends with the photography. Between both of my jobs and tight budgeting, I managed to pay off nearly two hundred thousand dollars in school loans by the time Drew passed all his certification exams."

"Jesus," I breathed, thoroughly impressed with her persistence and determination, even though I knew this story didn't have a happy ending.

"Drew was hired on as a full-time trauma surgeon at Cedars Sinai in Los Angeles, debt free." She smiled bitterly. "I wanted to get pregnant right away, but he wanted to wait a year for us to build up a nest egg so we could buy a house, so I continued working my two jobs. Six months later, Drew asked for a divorce. He'd been having an affair with a young, twenty-something nurse with bleached-blond hair and huge fake boobs. And, oh, Barbie—I kid you not about her name—was pregnant with his baby."

"*Fuck*," I muttered as my hands curled into fists I wished I could plant into Drew's face. After everything Kendall had done for him, the bastard had screwed her over. Ten years of her life wasted on a piece-of-shit guy who hadn't appreciated any of the sacrifices she'd made on his behalf. Selfish prick.

She shrugged, trying to act as though she was over her ex's betrayal, but the pain in her eyes was unmistakable. "To add insult to injury, I was stupid enough to ask why he'd had an affair, and what I'd done wrong. He told me he was bored, that I just didn't excite him sexually and he couldn't imagine spending the rest of his life with me."

A vein in my temple throbbed, and now her words to me made perfect sense—the huge age difference between us, and her fear that I'd get tired of her and move on to someone younger and more in line with my age. I wasn't wired like that—I was one hundred percent monoga-mous when it came to my relationships, and I'd always been far more attracted to older women because of their overall maturity. But proving any of that to Kendall would obviously take time and a helluva lot of patience considering how her ex had damaged her self-confidence and self-worth.

But there was one thing I could refute right

here, right now. I reached out and slid my hand around her legs, caressed my palms up the backs of her calves, and skimmed my fingers along that sensitive patch of skin behind her knee. Her eyes darkened with desire, and her skin flushed beautifully with renewed awareness.

"Your ex was a selfish asshole who obviously didn't try very hard to please *you* sexually, because you are far from boring," I stated firmly, truthfully. "If he would have given you what *you* needed and taken the time to learn your hottest fantasies like I did, he would have reaped the benefits of just how passionate and responsive you are."

She shook her head, wearing those doubts and insecurities right on her sleeve. "It doesn't matter."

"The hell it doesn't." Hating that one man had caused her so much pain and heartache, that Drew the dickwad had blamed Kendall for his own shortcomings, I did the only thing I knew that would erase all those doubts in her mind.

I moved so quickly, so unexpectedly, it took her a few extra seconds to realize what I was doing, but by then I already had her dress pushed up to her waist, her panties pulled off, and I was kneeling on the floor in front of her.

Her eyes were wide and startled, confused even, as she stared down at me. "Jase, what are you doing?"

"I'm showing you how Goddamn passionate you are," I said on a low, heated growl. With my hands hooked around the backs of her knees, I yanked her ass to the edge of the bed and lifted her legs over my shoulders, the abrupt, sudden movement causing her hips, her entire body actually, to tip backwards.

She gasped in shock, both of her arms shooting out behind her to steady herself just as I pressed my mouth to her gorgeous cunt and slid my tongue through those soft, swollen lips—licking, sucking, and consuming her completely. There was nothing sweet, tender, or romantic about the relentless way I went down on her, the ravenous, demanding way I ate her pussy and fucked her with my tongue. It was rough and crude and exceedingly, deliciously dirty.

I sucked hard on her clit, and she cried out, one of her hands reaching out to grip my hair in an attempt to pull my head away. She could yank out every strand and I wasn't leaving her or this luscious pussy, not until she gave me the orgasm I wanted. After a few more torturous licks and the surprising scrape of my teeth, she moaned, and those fingers changed direction, easing around the back of my head to bring me closer, to press my face harder between her thighs.

She fell back against the bed, giving herself over to the rising pleasure as she rocked her hips in rhythm to my stroking tongue and shamelessly rode my mouth. I pushed two fingers deep inside her and felt the immediate clench of her body, the internal contractions that rippled through her right before her orgasm peaked.

A hoarse scream tore from her throat. Her thighs shook and quivered, her back arched, and the hands in my hair twisted even tighter as she came so beautifully for me, so exquisitely, that there was no denying just how sensual and desirable she was.

With that issue proven, I turned my attention to obliterating her ex's other stupid-ass claims. I moved up and over Kendall's slack body, settled my hips between her spread thighs, and positioned the thick length of my rock-hard cock against the pussy I'd just thoroughly pleasured. If I hadn't been still wearing my slacks, I would have been balls deep inside her by now.

She stared up at me, her hands splayed on my chest, her gaze hazy but cautious after what I'd just done. I could feel the wet heat of her soaking into the front of my slacks and bit back a deep groan. This wasn't about me getting off. It was about showing Kendall exactly what kind of effect she had on me, how much I wanted her, and to make her forget that her ex had ever existed on the face of the planet.

"Does that fucking feel like I'm *bored*, Kendall?" I demanded, moving against her so she felt every steel inch of my throbbing dick. "Like you don't excite me?"

She made a startled noise in the back of her throat, her expression suddenly apprehensive, her body once again tense.

When she tried to look away, I pushed my fingers through her hair, turned her face back up to me, and held her gaze because I wasn't done getting everything out in the open. Wasn't done telling her the truth of what she did to me on all levels.

"You make me want to conquer and claim and possess you in the most primal way possible so there's no doubt in your mind that you belong to me," I said gruffly. "At the same time, you tempt me, entice me, and you make me so crazy with lust and the need to touch you, kiss you, and be so deep inside you that you're the only thing that matters. And *that's* what you deserve from a man. To feel nothing less than sexy and seductive, and to know that you have the power to bring him to his knees, just like you brought me to mine only minutes ago."

By the time I was finished, moisture and regret shimmered in her eyes. "Jase..." Her voice was an aching whisper. "I can't do this with you."

"Yes, you can. *Trust* me."

She shook her head and bit her bottom lip before speaking again. "I'm...I'm seeing some-one," she blurted out.

A chill coursed through my veins, as if I'd just been doused with ice water. Swearing beneath my breath, I stood up as my brain tried to process what she'd just said. She slowly sat up on the bed, eyeing me hesitantly after dropping that bombshell.

I'm seeing someone. I shoved my hand through my hair as my stomach churned. *She was seeing someone.* Another man. What the hell was there to fucking process?

I jammed my hands on my hips and narrowed my gaze. "If you're *seeing someone*, then why the hell are you here, at The Players Club?" Anger sharpened my tone.

She flinched at my harsh voice as she pushed the hem of her dress back down her legs. "Grant and I aren't exclusive," she said, mollifying me somewhat with her reply. "We met on an online dating site, and we've only been out together twice, but he's a good match." She sounded as though she was trying to convince herself of that fact.

A good match sounded so impersonal, so analytical. "If he was that great of a match, you wouldn't be here with me," I pointed out.

"I wasn't *supposed* to be here with you," she said quietly as she stood and put her panties back on again. "It was supposed to be a stranger. Someone who I didn't know, who I could have an anonymous fling with before things got serious with Grant."

Before things got serious, which meant that I still had a chance with her. "Stop seeing him."

I caught a flicker of anguish in her gaze before she looked away. "This—you and I—it's not going to work."

She attempted to walk around me to leave, and, feeling an odd sense of panic, I caught her arm to stop her. "You don't know that."

She looked up at me, her expression direct. "Are you at a point in your life where you're ready to get married?" she asked bluntly. "To settle down and have a family?"

Her unexpected questions took me aback, forcing me to switch mental gears so I could think about my answers. I definitely intended to get married someday and have kids, always had, but I'd only been out of the Air Force for a short time and was just starting to build my career with Noble and Associates as a security analyst.

I'd been an "accident" baby to my much-older parents, an unplanned child that they didn't know what to do with since they'd believed they were done raising kids. At the time, my two older sisters had been in their twenties, already graduated college, out on their own, and building their adult lives. My parents had downsized to a much smaller house and had been enjoying the freedom to travel when they wanted, to do things spontaneously, and not be tied to any set schedule. My mother, who'd always been a full-time housewife, had just graduated from culinary school as a pastry chef, which had always been a dream of hers.

And then *I'd* happened, and my parents' lives had been turned upside down by the unexpected pregnancy. Their newfound freedom hadn't accounted for the responsibilities and burdens of another child, and I'd felt the painful effects of that resentment growing up. Most of the time, I'd felt like a nuisance, an inconvenience, and was, essentially, an afterthought in my parents' lives and plans.

Knowing what it felt like to be an outcast as a child, I'd always had a certain vision for my future, a plan and strategy for my own life, including when and how children would fit in. I'd joined the military at the age of eighteen, intending to use my high-level computer skills in the Air Force to advance as a security systems specialist. Once I was done with my eight-year term, I'd focus on building my career with a strong, reputable security company and pad my savings for a few years. I wanted to be firmly established in every aspect of my life before I settled down and started a family, because I intended to be a hands-on dad and devote time and attention to raising my kids. I wanted my own children to have everything I'd grown up without.

So to answer Kendall's question, no, I wasn't near ready to get married and have babies. That was still a few years away and wasn't even on my personal radar yet. Which was exactly the point she was trying to make.

Fuck. Feeling like I'd just been kicked hard in the stomach, and knowing I couldn't make those promises right now, I released my hold on her.

She rubbed her arms, and the small smile she gave me was sad, understanding even. "It's okay," she said softly. "You're young and you're not ready for that kind of life and responsibilities. But I am, and so is Grant. He's a nice guy, and we have a lot in common, which we already knew based on the online profile we both had to fill out. We're both established in our careers, we're the same age, and we have the same future goals. I'm not getting any younger, and I really want a family and kids. It's all I've wanted for years."

And her rat bastard ex had stolen that from her in the worst way possible. What Kendall wanted, what she *deserved*, was a man who would give her all those things. Even though I couldn't make that kind of commitment to her, I didn't want to let her go, either. And the thought of another man touching her in any way made me resentful as hell.

How selfish of an asshole did that make *me*?

I had no reply that didn't make me sound like said asshole, so I kept my jaw clenched tight and my mouth shut, even though it nearly killed me to do so.

She reached up and laid her palm against my cheek, then gave me a smile so sweet that it made the heart in my chest constrict so tight it hurt to breathe. "You gave me the most erotic night of my life tonight," she said huskily, her face still flushed from that last orgasm I'd given her. "Thank you for that."

I didn't want Kendall's fucking gratitude. I wanted *her*. So badly that, when she walked out the door, I felt as though she'd taken a part of me with her that I'd never be able to get back.

CHAPTER 7

Kendall

I glanced at the handsome chiropractor sitting across the small table from me, his gaze quite serious as he perused the bar's wine list through his reading glasses. "They really don't have a very big selection of good wine here," Grant said, sounding disappointed even as he glanced up at me and asked, "Which would you prefer? Red Zinfandel or the Chardonnay?"

"Neither," I said, which earned me a startled look from Grant. "I'm not much of a wine drinker," I quickly explained. To me, all wines, expensive or cheap, seemed to taste the same—tart and tangy. It just wasn't my thing. "I think I'm going to have a lemon drop martini."

He frowned at me over the black rim of his glasses. "It's a shame you don't care for wine. I have a small cellar at home with bottles of great wine, and I belong to the Wine of the Month Club."

"Ahh, more wine for you, then," I teased, but he didn't even crack a smile. He obviously took his wine very seriously.

He went back to his wine list, which gave me a few more minutes to just sit back in my chair and relax. This was my third outing with Grant—the first had been coffee at Starbucks with easy conversation and the second an informal lunch that had ended with a nice kiss. This was our first evening date, and I'd agreed to meet him at the small, casual bar and grill a few miles from my studio after we'd finished work for the day.

He'd offered to pick me up at home, but I wasn't quite ready for that next step. Him knowing where I lived made things more inti-mate, and I wasn't ready to deal with that awkward *should I invite him in for coffee or not* scenario when he dropped me off at the end of the date.

As a chiropractor who worked in an office setting, he wore a nice dress shirt and tie and slacks. His sandy-blond hair was cut short, his jaw clean shaven even though it was after six in the evening. He was well put together, success-ful, and he acted like a gentleman. We could carry on an intelligent conversation about world events, though he always seemed uncomfortable when I talked about my boudoir photography. I knew what I did for a living was unusual, and figured he just needed to wrap his mind around the fact that I took pictures of women in lingerie and men in their briefs.

Like Jase in his briefs, then nothing at all.

I almost groaned at the inappropriate thought that popped into my head, but then again, since my night with him the previous weekend, I'd found it difficult to *stop* thinking about him. And fantasizing about him. And remembering all the hot, dirty, erotic things he'd done to me. Those sexy, provocative images were forever branded in my mind, a reminder of what I'd walked away from and given up.

It had been the right thing to do, for the both of us. And I'd been telling myself that excuse every day since.

Yet I couldn't help but think how ironic it was that I'd gone ten years with bland, vanilla sex, another two long years without sex, then *finally* had the absolute best and most orgasmic sex of my life when I'd finally given up on ever experiencing that kind of passion. And now I was at a point in my life when it was more important for me to find a man who'd be a good husband and father, and *not* a man who could rock my world, make my deepest, most forbidden fantasies a reality, and use his tongue in ways I'd never imagined but had absolutely loved.

As if I could feel that wicked tongue of his sliding between my thighs, I shivered and squirmed in my chair.

Grant set the wine list down on the table and looked over at me again, concern in his gaze. "Are you cold? Do you want me to go get my sports jacket from my car?"

My date was so attentive and thoughtful,

while my mind had been back at The Players Club with another man. Dammit, I really needed to stop thinking about Jase. "No, I'm fine," I said to Grant and smiled.

Our waiter came by, and Grant ordered our drinks—the Zinfandel for him and a lemon drop martini for me.

"What can I get the two of you for dinner tonight?" the young man asked.

Both men were looking at me—polite and considerate, ladies first—so I placed my order. "I'll have the pasta carbonara."

"Are you sure you don't want to get one of the grilled seafood entrees?" Grant asked seriously. "It's a much healthier choice."

I blinked at him. I hadn't seen *that* coming. I knew Grant was health conscious and liked to run, including marathons. Yes, I hated running, but I did yoga three times a week and watched what I ate for the most part. But when I had a meal out, which wasn't all that often since I was single, I liked to indulge.

I gave him a decisive look. "No, I'll take the pasta."

He finally glanced back at the waiter. "I'll

have the grilled shrimp and steamed vegetables."

Once the young man left, Grant braced his arms on the table and raised a disapproving brow my way. "You know you're going to have to spend an extra half hour on the treadmill to burn off all those excess carbs, right?"

I resisted the urge to laugh but knew Grant wasn't kidding. "I don't have a treadmill."

"That's not a problem," he said, and flashed me a pleased smile as he shared his brilliant idea. "I'll set you up with a membership at my gym, and we can go together."

Now that sounded like fun. Not. I didn't begrudge Grant's routine of working out, respected it even, but sweating in a gym held no appeal to me. "I think I'll stick to my yoga sessions."

"Then you might want to watch those carbs," he said with a wink.

The waiter came to our table at that moment to deliver our drinks, saving me from having to reply. I took a big drink of my lemon drop martini while Grant swirled his Zinfandel in his glass and sniffed the contents before tasting the wine.

I thought our health and fitness discussion was done, but Grant launched into a spiel about a new all-natural dietary supplement he was offering to his clients who were looking to improve their energy and lifestyle, and for me, he'd sell it at his cost. I thanked him and declined and took another drink of my martini.

When our meals arrived, he enthusiastically continued his sales pitch, talking about amino acids, minerals, antioxidants, and all the benefits of this all-natural supplement—better digestion, tissue repair, disease prevention, and most importantly, those vitamins worked to neutralize free radical chemicals that caused oxidative damage in human cells.

What the hell was a free radical chemical? All the information was enough to make my head spin and my eyes glaze over. Since he was on a roll, all I could do was nod every once in a while as if I actually understood what he was talking about—because I didn't want to be rude and flat-out tell him he was boring me to the point that I needed another drink.

Nowhere on his online profile had he mentioned being a health nut, which wasn't a bad thing. It just wasn't *my* thing. Our compatibility Q and A had matched us as having common beliefs and core values. We were the same age. We both wanted a family. We each had a stable and successful career. We had the same political views, and religion wasn't an issue for either of us. We both preferred committed relationships instead of dating around.

On the surface, when it came to our fundamental beliefs, we were extremely well suited. But I'd yet to find a connection when it came to our personal interests or leisure activities, and this evening with him brought that to light. There wasn't a strong physical attraction on my side, and while I knew better than to expect butterflies and fireworks with him—and especially not the kind of passion I'd experienced with Jase—it was the whole package that made me realize that Grant just wasn't *the one*.

I liked Grant. He was a genuinely nice guy despite his quirks, but I just didn't see myself with him long term. And it wasn't fair to him for me to continue seeing him after tonight.

Grant's cell phone buzzed on the table, and

he glanced at the caller ID, then gave me an apologetic look as he stood up with his phone in hand. "I've been expecting this call. I need to talk to a colleague about a charity golf tournament that's coming up. I'll be back in a few minutes."

Golfing. One more thing I had absolutely no interest in. "Go right ahead," I said, and watched him walk out into the lobby area as he answered the call. As soon as he was gone, I breathed easier. Another sign that we just weren't going to work out.

Finished with my dinner, I set my fork on my plate and waited for him to return. My cell phone, also on the table, buzzed and lit up. Not with a call but a text message from Jase. Just seeing his name for the first time since *that night* made my stomach execute a little flip of awareness, and I unlocked my phone to read his note.

You look gorgeous in that pretty pink lace dress you're wearing.

The comment startled me because I *was* wearing a pale pink lace-lined dress. Frowning, I glanced around where I was sitting in the dining area. Most of the tables were full, but I didn't see Jase anywhere.

I typed in a reply. *How would you know what I'm wearing?*

Because I've been watching you for the past thirty minutes.

I shivered at the thought. *Where are you?*

In the lounge area, sitting at the far end of the bar having a beer and a burger. Look up, to your left, and through the partition separating the bar from the dining area.

I did, and finally saw him, tucked away in a shadowed corner. He tipped his beer bottle in my direction in greeting, and I couldn't stop the smile that tugged at the corner of my mouth or the butterflies fluttering to life in my belly. *Damn.*

Are you stalking me? I teased.

I have dinner here occasionally. Just so happens you were here tonight with him. I swear I'm not stalking you, but I am lusting after you. Always will.

A swell of emotion rushed through me, and he continued before I replied.

I wish I was sitting next to you right now. You can bet my hand would be under your dress and stroking along the insides of your thighs, and higher, until my fingers were brushing bare, naked flesh.

I clenched my legs together. A groan rose up in my throat, and I swallowed it back. I wasn't sure how to reply to something so intimate and erotic, so I didn't.

But that didn't stop him from tormenting me further. *I can still remember how soft and wet you got when I touched you, how it felt to have your hands twisting in my hair as I went down on you. You tasted like peaches. Ripe, juicy, and sweet.*

My heart raced in my chest, my face flushed, and I wet my suddenly dry lips with my tongue. Logically, I knew I should stop his sexting, knew all this was so inappropriate when I was on a date with another man, but I couldn't look away when he sent another message.

Lick your lips like that again. Slowly.

As if he had complete control over my actions, I met his gaze from across the dining room and bar area and did as he asked.

I watched as his jaw clenched and his eyes flared with heat before he glanced down at his phone and sent me another text.

I am so fucking hard right now. I want your hot mouth on my cock and my tongue on your pussy. At the same time.

His wickedly dirty suggestion jolted through me and flooded my entire body with desire and need. The image of me engaging in that sixty-nine position with Jase was now emblazoned in my mind and would no doubt be a staple in my nightly fantasies.

I fucking hate seeing you with him.

Jase's words and the heartfelt emotion in them cut through me like a knife, because I knew the sentiment was real and sincere. And what could I say to that? *I know? I'm sorry? It's best this way because long term isn't in our future?*

"I apologize for taking so long on that call," Grant said, startling me as he returned to the table and slid back into the seat across from me.

I quickly turned off my phone and put it into my purse. Out of sight, out of mind. *Yeah, right.* Jase hadn't left my thoughts since I'd left the club nearly a week ago. "Is everything okay with the charity event?" I asked Grant.

He shook his head, his frustration evident. "No. I'm on the committee to recruit sponsors for the golf tournament, and we had one of the major brands just pull out when the event is only a few weeks away. Getting someone this late in the game to fund and promote the event is going to be next to impossible." He waved a dismissive hand in the air. "But enough about that. I don't want to ruin the evening with me ranting about something that can't be changed right this moment."

No, instead I was going to ruin *his* evening when I ended things with him. And yeah, I felt really bad about that. But I refused to lead him on or give him false hopes about the two of us.

The waiter came by to clear away our dinner plates. "Can I get you two dessert tonight?"

Without even asking me if I might be interested in their chocolate mousse, cheesecake, or anything else from their after-dinner menu, Grant shook his head. "No, thank you. Just the check please."

I wasn't going to order dessert, not when I knew how this evening was going to end, but the fact that Grant hadn't even given me a choice—probably because he'd been counting the carbs, fat, and calories in my pasta dish—

helped to further solidify my decision to move on.

I wasn't giving up my dessert or sweets for any man.

Once the bill was paid, we stood up, and Grant ushered me toward the front of the restaurant with his hand low on my back. As we passed the bar area, I didn't look in Jase's direction, though I felt his gaze on me, anyway.

Once we were outside, Grant walked me toward my car. When we reached the driver's side, I turned around to face him, to do what needed to be done.

Except he pushed his hands into the front pockets of his slacks and spoke first. "I was thinking…maybe you and I could go on a day trip this weekend to Solvang and stop at some of the wineries for a tour and tasting. I'm hoping to show you what you're missing out on." He grinned at me.

The idea didn't appeal to me in any way. I shook my head, exhaled a deep breath, and got right to the point. "Grant…you're a really great guy, but I don't think you and I are going to work out."

His smile fell away, and I felt horrible.

"Why don't you think we'll work out?" he asked, genuinely confused. "I thought we hit it off pretty well. And our online profiles showed us as extremely compatible."

Practically and logically, yes, we'd been a good match. But personally and individually, and connecting on a deeper level, not so much. Grant was the first guy I'd gone out with from the dating site and since my divorce, and as much as I'd wanted things to work out, I realized I needed...more.

"It's just not the right fit for me," I said honestly. I was tempted to say *it's not you, it's me*, but didn't think he'd appreciate the cliché, even if it was the truth. "I'm sure you'll find the right woman for you, one who'll appreciate your wine cellar," I said, trying a bit of humor to break up the awkward tension.

It worked. He glanced at me sheepishly. "You're probably right. I'm very analytical, and I think I got too caught up in the compatibility results." He hesitated for a moment, then said, "I've actually been emailing with another woman I met on the dating site who enjoys a good bottle of Cabernet Sauvignon. I think I'll see if she wants to take that day trip to Solvang with me."

"That's a *great* idea," I said, relieved that there were no hard feelings between us.

"I hope we can still be friends?" he asked.

I nodded. "Of course."

He finally grinned. "If you ever need your back adjusted or want to give those supplements a try, just give my office a call. I'll still sell them to you for my cost."

I managed not to laugh, because he was so serious about his offer. "I appreciate that."

"I really enjoyed meeting you, and I hope you find what you're looking for." He leaned forward and placed a quick, chaste kiss on my cheek. "Good night, Kendall."

He waited until I got into my car and locked the door before he walked to his. Even after he left the parking lot, I sat in my vehicle, reluctant to leave, and I knew exactly why—because I still wanted the man inside the restaurant and no one else. And until I got my fill of passion and pleasure and worked Jase out of my system, it was impossible for me to focus on the future.

I wasn't giving up my dreams of having a

stable marriage and starting a family, I was just allowing myself to enjoy some sexy fun, guilt-free. A few weeks of being uninhibited and even a little brazen. Daring and adventurous. No modesty, no limits, no insecurities.

I was going to be naughty and bad.

Very, very bad, I thought with a grin.

So bad I might even need a spanking.

I laughed out loud, feeling lighter and more carefree than I had in a long time. I wasn't sure what the future held for me, but two things were absolutely certain right now.

I wanted Jase, and I wanted my dessert.

CHAPTER 8

Jase

I was so fucking pathetic.

I shoved my half-eaten burger across the bar, my appetite vanishing as I'd watched Kendall walk out of the restaurant with her date—a successful, stable, respectable-looking guy who she claimed to have everything in common with and who could quite possibly give her that future she was searching for. A future she one hundred percent deserved.

Jealousy—an emotion I wasn't at all familiar

with when it came to women—nearly strangled me. I jammed a hand through my hair and swore beneath my breath, hating that she'd left with the other man, that the guy had the right to touch Kendall when I no longer did or could.

More resentment stirred in my belly and ate at me like an ulcer. I'd never felt this way about any other woman I'd dated, or even Cheryl, who I'd had a year-and-a-half relationship with while we'd both been in the Air Force. Even when she'd ended things, I'd understood her reasons, and it had been easy to let her go. No emotional turmoil, no drama, no hurt feelings, no goddamn jealousy or cynicism.

Yet having to witness Kendall leave with Mr. Perfect, and imagining how they might spend their evening, was enough to make me want to punch a hole in the nearest wall, and I so wasn't a violent person.

"Can I get you anything else, hot stuff?" Mallory, the female bartender, asked me as she picked up my plate and set it in a bin under the counter.

In the few weeks that I'd been coming here,

I always sat at the bar, and Mallory always flirted with me. She was young and pretty, and she'd made it clear on more than one occasion that she was interested in me. But since meeting Kendall, it was as though I had blinders on when it came to other women. And now knowing what it felt like to be inside of her, to have her come apart beneath me, I wasn't sure anyone else could compare or satisfy me.

Yeah, I was fucking pathetic.

I was just about to ask for another beer, or maybe something stronger to drown my misery, when I saw Kendall walk back into the restaurant. She veered toward the lounge area and headed in my direction. Her stride in those sexy, white strappy high heels was purposeful. Determined. Confident. There was a sensual sway to her hips as she walked, and while the pink lace dress skimmed her body in a sweet, modest way, the smile on her lips was far from innocent as she approached.

The woman heading my way was different from the one who'd just left. Hell, this woman was different from any version I'd ever seen of Kendall, and I was intrigued. And hopeful, even though I was probably setting myself up for a huge disappointment.

I had no idea why she'd returned sans her date, but a crazy anticipation filled me, and I couldn't tear my gaze away, too afraid the gorgeous vision of her would disappear if I even blinked.

"I'm good right now," I finally said to Mallory. "Real good."

I hadn't meant to speak the latter out loud, but my comment made the bartender curious enough to follow my gaze to see what had so thoroughly captured my attention.

"Lucky girl," Mallory said with an envious sigh before walking away to fill another drink order.

No, not a girl. A *woman*, I silently amended, because that's what Kendall was. Mature, intelligent, and at thirty-five, she was in her sexual prime. Her breasts were small but firm, and real. She was soft and curvy in all the right places, and as she neared, my body responded, tightened, and my heart beat a little faster. Jesus, I was completely and utterly infatuated with her.

She slid into the vacant chair beside me, so

close that her thigh pressed against mine. I ignored the flash of heat that simple touch caused, and asked the obvious question.

"Where's your date?"

"Gone." She met my gaze and exhaled a deep breath. "Grant and I are done."

"Done?" I knew I probably sounded like I was dense, but I needed her to explain exactly what *done* meant before I let myself get too excited and optimistic.

"We're finished." She shrugged, causing her soft, loose curls to brush across her shoulder. "No more dating. We're going our separate ways."

"Why?" I asked cautiously.

A cute smile tugged up the corners of her full pink lips, and her eyes danced with humor. "Because no man comes between me and my dessert."

My mouth twitched with amusement. I loved this lighthearted side to Kendall, and while I knew her reasons for breaking things off with Grant probably went much deeper, I played along for now. "He wouldn't let you have dessert?" I raised a scandalous brow. "The bastard."

"Exactly," she said, and laughed, the sound fun and engaging. "And he was very concerned about how I was going to burn off the extra calories from the pasta I had for dinner. He even offered to get me a membership at his gym."

Oh, yeah, the guy had totally sealed his own fate. Not that I was complaining, considering Kendall was now sitting next to me, relaxed and more carefree than she'd ever been with me before when she was normally so composed, guarded, and reserved.

And because she was being so playful, I decided to test the waters and do the same. I placed a hand on her knee and stroked my fingers just above the hem of her dress in a teasing caress. "Instead of working out at a gym, I know a much more effective and enjoyable way to burn off those extra calories."

She turned her body more fully toward mine, allowing my hand to slip farther beneath her dress. "Yeah?" she asked, the daring look in her eyes blowing me away. "Like what?"

Oh, she was feisty. And I loved this new brazen attitude that made her so irresistible and sexy as hell. We were tucked away in the corner of the bar, looking as though we were having an intimate conversation. Which we were, but it was about to get a whole lot more seductive.

Giving her a wicked grin, I leaned in closer and grazed the tips of my fingers a bit higher, enjoying the feel of her soft, smooth skin. "Like you straddling my hips and riding my cock and getting all hot and sweaty," I murmured, watching as her gaze darkened with desire while her legs eased open a little wider, inviting my hand farther. "It's also a great exercise to work out the muscles in your thighs and your abdomen, and you get the bonus of releasing tension with an orgasm."

She bit her bottom lip as my fingers reached the apex of her legs and stroked along the damp crotch of her panties. A palpable tremor coursed through her, and she tipped her head to the side so that her hair hid her flushed face from everyone but me.

"I think I like your workout regimen *much* better than his," she said breathlessly.

I pushed a finger against her clit and rubbed against the drenched fabric. A tiny moan escaped her, and my dick swelled painfully against the front closure of my jeans. "You're already so fucking wet," I murmured. It was all I could do to resist the impulse to pull her astride my lap and start that *workout regimen* right this second.

She laughed huskily. "That happened when you texted me and told me you wanted my mouth sucking your cock with your tongue between my legs at the same time."

The quote wasn't word for word, but the sentiment was the same. "I *do* want that with you."

My reply was direct, my desire for her undisguised. I expected her to retreat, but she didn't move away. Didn't shut down or put up those too-high walls that seemed impossible for me to scale. No, this confident new woman looked me straight in the eyes and nearly knocked me into another dimension with her response.

"I want that, too."

Mind fucking blown. At a temporary loss for words, I stared at her to try and read her expression, but then out of the corner of my eye, I caught Mallory heading back down to our end of the bar. Very slowly, I removed my hand from beneath Kendall's dress, just as the bartender reached us.

"Would you like something to drink?" she asked Kendall.

I watched Kendall gather her composure and smile at the other woman. "Yes. I'll have a large glass of milk."

Mallory blinked at her in confusion. "Did you say milk?"

Kendall nodded. "Yes. And I'd like a slice of your double chocolate fudge cake to go with it."

The bartender laughed. "Ahhh, a woman after my own heart. I'd take chocolate cake over alcohol any day."

Mallory moved away to place the order, and I grinned at Kendall.

"A double chocolate fudge cake," I said, and shook my head. "You don't mess around with your desserts, do you?"

"Nope." Her expression softened, and her gaze turned serious. "I think I'm beginning to realize that life is too short, and you just need to go for it sometimes and indulge."

I got the distinct impression that she was referring to more than just the dessert. Which brought my thoughts back around to the man she'd just ended things with, and what it meant for the two of us.

"Why did you come back in here?" I asked.

She crossed one leg over the other and gave me a resigned smile. "I came back in here to tell you that you won."

I frowned, not sure what to make of that. "What have I won?"

"This. Us." She waved a hand between us, then absently worried her bottom lip. "Obviously, that one night with you at The Players Club wasn't enough for me. I still want you, and it's interfering with my ability to focus on any other man."

I managed not to grin like a fool at her confession, yet I needed a more specific explanation from her. "So, what are you saying, exactly?"

She tapped her fingers anxiously on the bar top. "I'm saying…let's get this crazy attraction we have for one another out of our systems, so we can each go our separate ways and move on with our normal lives."

Ahhh, so those walls of hers weren't gone, after all. She was merely lowering them for a *fling*, while separating anything emotional from what she wanted from me physically. Basically, she was suggesting an affair, a friends-with-benefits kind of situation that was casual and discreet and wouldn't involve any kind of complicated feelings. She was offering me a man's ultimate dream scenario— sex without commitment.

That might work for some guys but not for me. I wanted more from her. Hell, I might even want it all. The revelation was huge, but I didn't fight it.

I placed my hand over hers, stopping her nervous fidgeting. "So, you want to use me for sex?" I teased.

Her face flushed, contradicting the naughty smile on her lips. "I think it would be a mutually satisfying proposition. But I wouldn't want you to do anything you didn't want to."

No, it certainly wouldn't be a hardship to have Kendall naked and moaning beneath me. There wasn't anything I didn't want to do to her and with her. And if this fling was all I could have of her right now, then I'd take it. I wasn't ready to let her go, and I sure as hell didn't want her finding another man to scratch that itch. I'd figure out everything else later.

Hopefully she'd come to realize that kind of empty affair wasn't enough. I planned to do everything in my power to help her come to that conclusion.

I gently turned her hand over and stroked my fingers along her palm, watching the rise and fall of her chest as I touched her. "I think I can handle being a sex object for you."

"I want…" Her voice was suddenly low and raspy, her fingers starting their twitching again. "I want more of what we did at The Players Club." She hesitated once more, met my gaze, then spoke. "This is hard for me, but I'm going to be honest. Sex wasn't all that great in my marriage. I thought it was because we were both so busy, with me working two jobs, and his schooling and internship. It was all very vanilla, mostly missionary, and nothing out of the ordinary or even adventurous."

"No passion," I murmured.

"No, no, passion," she agreed with a small shake of her head. "And I was fine with that because it was really all I knew." More quietly, she added, "And because I didn't know what I was missing until that night with you at the club. Now I want more of that."

I quickly glanced around the bar area to make sure we were alone, that nobody could overhear our conversation, before I asked, "More of what, exactly?"

"Being taken. Restrained. Spanked," she said in a hushed tone, even as the pulse at the base of her neck began a rapid beat. "I want to be pushed beyond conventional sexual boundaries. I want to be fucked hard. I like it when you're aggressive and demanding. When you pull my hair and make me do naughty, wicked things."

Holy shit. I couldn't stop staring at her mouth, couldn't stop thinking about all those naughty, wicked things I could make her do with it. *Stroke. Lick. Suck.* My cock twitched, hardened, totally on board with every filthy fantasy that drifted through my mind.

"And before I start dating again," she went on, jarring me out of my dirty thoughts, "I want to experience all that and more."

Before I start dating again. Those words were like a bucket of ice water being dumped in my lap, even as another fierce, more possessive emotion rose to the surface. "I will fulfill every single desire you have, any way you want it," I promised. "But from this moment forward, you and I are exclusive, and you're mine. No online dating, no searching through profiles for that perfect guy who's your age and is looking for the same things as you are. Just you and me."

"Okay," she agreed easily enough. Then she cracked a wry smile and shook her head. "I never thought I'd become a cougar."

An older woman seducing a younger man. I knew the eight-year age difference was an issue for her, but it wasn't something I could change. But if I showed her that we were compatible outside of the bedroom, maybe she'd stop thinking in terms of me being so much younger than her, and all the issues she had with it personally.

That was my plan, anyway.

"You're not a cougar," I said as I tucked a few of those soft curls behind her ear before skimming the pad of my thumb along her jaw. "You're a puma."

"A puma?" she asked, laughter brimming in her voice. "What's that?"

"A cougar is a woman in her forties who dates a man at least twenty years younger than she is. A puma is a woman in her thirties who dates a guy in his twenties. So really, the age difference isn't all that bad." I grinned.

She rolled her eyes, unconvinced, though her gaze danced with humor. "Oh, being a puma makes it *so* much better."

I chuckled. "A puma is graceful and sleek and majestic. Not a bad thing to be compared to."

She tossed me a sassy look. "If you pet me, I might even purr."

I was tempted to do just that, but before I could follow through on the impulse and slip my hand beneath her dress again, we were interrupted.

"I am *so* sorry for the wait on your dessert," Mallory said as she rushed to our end of the bar, a plate with a slice of chocolate cake on it in one hand and a large glass of milk in the other. "The restaurant suddenly got busy and the drink orders at the bar are getting crazy."

"No problem," Kendall said as the younger girl set the dessert and drink down in front of her. "Thank you."

"You bet. Enjoy," Mallory said, then was gone again.

Kendall didn't waste any time in picking up

her fork and taking a bite of the cake, which looked moist and fudgy. She closed her eyes as she savored the taste and let out a soft, appreciative "mmm" in the back of her throat as she swallowed.

Damn. "I envy that cake right now," I said, and I wasn't kidding.

She opened her eyes and grinned at me, looking young and beautiful. "It's amazing and worth every calorie," she declared shamelessly. "Want a bite?"

She held a forkful up to my mouth, and I let her feed me the sample. The taste was rich, the texture gooey, and it surprisingly reminded me of home. "Yeah, that's pretty damn good."

"Right?" She picked up her glass of milk and took a drink.

Had I ever seen a woman enjoy dessert so much? If so, I couldn't remember when, and it was so easy to take pleasure in *her* simple pleasure. *This* was what I wanted with Kendall. These moments that made me feel good, in a way that had nothing to do with sex. Just being happy and content in the moment.

"That cake reminds me of my mother," I

said, the words coming out of my mouth on their own, without conscious thought.

"Yeah?" She tipped her head to the side. "Why is that?"

I hadn't meant to bring up my family, but since I had, I answered Kendall's question. "My mom was a pastry chef, and she made some really great desserts. Chocolate was her specialty." She'd also used those sweets as a substitution for affection, and to make up for the fact that she was rarely home. Not the greatest childhood memories.

"Oh." Kendall's eyes lit up with interest. "What a great job to have, but you used the word *was*, so I'm assuming she isn't a pastry chef any longer?"

"No, she's retired. So is my dad."

She stared at me for a few moments, and I knew she was taking my young age into consideration, and it wasn't all adding up. "Aren't your parents a bit young to retire yet?"

"No. My mom is seventy-three, and my dad is seventy-six. They've been retired for a while now."

She set her fork on her plate, and again, I could see the wheels turning in her mind as she did the logical math in her head. "Are you…adopted?"

A lot of people came to the same conclusion when they saw me with my parents. Or they thought that my mom and dad were actually my grandparents. "No. Not adopted. I was an accident."

She glanced at me in confusion. "An accident?"

"I wasn't planned," I explained as I used my thumb to wipe away a smear of frosting from the corner of her mouth. I'd much rather kiss her to distract her from this uncomfortable conversation but licked the chocolate from my finger instead. If I wanted more with Kendall, then that meant sharing even the most painful aspects of my life with her, along with the raw, honest truth of it.

"My mother was forty-six when she found out she was pregnant with me. My parents were done having kids, and I was definitely not planned in any way. Both of my older sisters, who were twenty-three and twenty-five at the time, were already out of college and out of the house."

"Oh, wow," she said, her eyes wide. "How

did it happen? I mean, I *know* how babies are made, of course…" She shook her head with a laugh. "You know what I'm getting at."

I did, and it was a curious question a lot of people asked, given how old my parents were when they'd conceived me. "My dad had a vasectomy after my second sister was born, so to find out they were pregnant with me was a huge surprise. Come to find out, his tubes grew back together over time. It's called recanalization, and the chances of it happening are extremely low, but here I am, proof that it does happen."

Her green eyes danced playfully. "I'm sure you were a *good* kind of surprise."

"No…not so much." I watched her expression go from amusement to shock, and her lips parted in disbelief. "My parents, at their age, didn't really want another child. After already raising two daughters who were grown adults, they thought they were done with diapers and nightly feedings and toddler tantrums. They'd just downsized to a two-bedroom house and had planned on doing all the traveling they hadn't been able to do while my sisters were young. I was definitely an inconvenience for them, an annoyance that made it difficult for them to do the things they'd planned on before I came along."

Kendall winced, her gaze sympathetic. "Is that why you joined the military? So you could leave home when you graduated high school?"

"Yep," I said with a nod. "Growing up, I had a ton of different babysitters until I was old enough to be left alone, so I learned to be independent and self-sufficient at a young age. By the time I was ten, I was cooking my own meals, washing my own clothes, and was pretty much by myself during the day and early evenings. Materialistically—clothes, food, a roof over my head—they made sure I had everything a child needed. But emotionally, for the most part, I was an afterthought."

"I'm so sorry, Jase," she said softly, her features etched with compassion.

I shrugged, having come to terms with my unconventional childhood long ago. There was nothing I could do to change the past, but I knew I wouldn't repeat my parents' mistakes when it came to my own kids. They would always know that they were loved unconditionally, and that they were one of the most important things in my life.

"It is what it is," I said with a small quirk of my lips. "I went into the Air Force because I knew exactly what I wanted to do, which involved computers and security. When I was a teenager, my parents bought me this elaborate computer system so I'd have something to do while they were at work, or not home, and that's how I spent most of my time. I became really fascinated by the military's computer network operations. Specifically cyber attack and defenses, and how to leverage and optimize those network operations in warfare," I said, not going into depth or detail since I knew she'd never understand the terminology.

A slight frown creased her brows. "That sounds so complicated," she said, proving my point as she ate another bite of her cake.

"I was a techie computer nerd growing up, so I loved all that cyber stuff. I still am a nerd," I said humorously.

"You are so *not* a nerd," she said with a roll of her eyes before bringing the discussion back to my family. "So, do your parents and sisters live around here?"

"No. They all live in South Carolina. That's where I was born and raised."

"Yet you live here in San Diego?"

I shrugged. "I really like everything about Southern California. The sun, the beach, the laid-back vibe. I'm happy with my job at Noble and Associates, I have great friends here, so it's a perfect place for me to live." I'd never felt those ties to my parents, and I wasn't close to my sisters, so it had been easy for me to relocate somewhere else once I left the military. This was where I wanted to build my future.

"What about your family?" I asked, wanting to know about her, too.

She took a sip of her milk and absently swiped her tongue along her bottom lip to lick up any excess moisture. "My parents live in Delaware, not yet retired, and I have a brother who lives in Connecticut with his wife and two little girls."

"Yet you live here in Southern California, as well," I repeated back to her.

She looked away, but not before I saw the flash of pain in her eyes. "Yeah, well, you know how all that came about," she said.

Yes, I did. She'd moved out to California to

go to college, met her dickhead ex-husband there, put him through med school and worked two jobs to pay all their accumulated debt, then he'd divorced her to marry some bimbo who was pregnant with his kid.

Asshole, I thought, and hoped I never came face-to-face with the prick, because I'd beat the shit out of him for hurting Kendall so badly.

After doing major damage to the chocolate cake, she'd pushed her plate away. Her hand was resting on the bar top, not fidgeting or nervous this time, but I gave in to the urge to pick it up and lace our fingers together, palm to palm. She didn't pull away, and I reveled in that bit of affection and acceptance.

"You lived in Los Angeles with…him," I said, loathe to say his actual name out loud. "So how did you end up here in San Diego?"

Now that she was done with her dessert, she turned toward me on the chair. I did the same but didn't let go of her hand. I liked the physical connection. A lot. The contact was intimate and caring without being smothering, and when Kendall looked at me with those big green eyes that were filled with a hint of vulnerability, I felt my chest constrict with a tenderness that was foreign to me.

I wanted to protect Kendall from any other hurt. Shield her from the kind of pain that left deep scars and made it hard for her to trust again. Unfortunately, it was too late to shelter her from the emotional wreckage her selfish ex had left in the aftermath of his narcissism. No, that would take time. And patience.

Luckily, I had plenty of both.

Just when I thought she wasn't going to answer my question, she replied quietly. "Well, after the divorce papers were signed and everything was split up, the one thing I knew was that I didn't want to be anywhere near Drew. I didn't want to accidentally run into him somewhere, or see Barbie pregnant with his baby when it should have been me." She glanced down at our joined hands, then back up at me with a half smile. "I wanted to start somewhere fresh and new, and I'd been to San Diego on a photo shoot I did for a family reunion. I fell in love with it here. So, I quit my job at the ad agency, I found a small one-bedroom apartment here, and started a whole new business."

"Your boudoir photography?"

She nodded, a glimmer of pride in her expression. "Yep. At first, I had to supplement my income with portrait photography, but once I found the studio I have now and I was able to get the right decor and furnishings for the boudoir settings, things just really took off."

I heard the excitement in her voice and grinned, loving how passionate she was about her job. How passionate *she was*, period.

"And then I met Raina, who, as you know, owns Sugar and Spice," she went on enthusiastically. "She started referring customers to me, and that's been huge, too, in building my clientele."

I absently skimmed my thumb across the back of her hand. "Why boudoir photography?" I had a feeling I knew the answer but wanted to hear it from her.

"I want to empower women to feel sexy and sensual and confident, no matter their size or shape," she told me, confirming what I'd already suspected. "I love seeing the transformation as I'm taking the pictures, watching these women go from shy and timid to being bold and radiant and uninhibited."

Did she even realize she was describing herself? That with me, she was becoming that sexy, fearless, self-assured woman she was talking about? She was like a sensual butterfly who'd just emerged from her cocoon, free and unfettered and wanting to experience all the erotic pleasures she'd missed out on.

And I was the lucky man to give her all that.

As I sat there and listened to her talk about her business, I realized that, without a doubt, I wanted more than easy sex with her, which contradicted her own request for a casual relationship. Which also meant I had to find some kind of balance, a way to get what I wanted while giving her what she desired and, in the process, building her trust and allaying her fears.

Not an easy feat, but I was determined to find a way, because there was one thing I knew with certainty: she was worth having in my life.

CHAPTER 9

Kendall

I couldn't believe how much I'd rambled on about Pure Bliss, but Jase had remained engaged and focused on me. He hadn't hesitated to ask questions, and it was nice to have a man who actually appreciated what I did for a living. A man who showed genuine interest in my photography business and wanted to know all about it.

Since returning to the bar, I'd spent nearly an hour and a half with Jase, and there hadn't been any lag in conversation. No awkward silences like I'd experienced with Grant. Jase hadn't made any derogatory comments about the chocolate cake I'd ordered—that would have been a deal breaker, for sure. We'd talked about our families, and my heart truly hurt for him and the less-than-ideal childhood he'd endured. I couldn't imagine how difficult it must have been for him to grow up alone and on his own, yet he'd become a competent, confident man who'd focused on his goals in life and made them happen.

Jase was the first man I'd ever opened up to and told about my lackluster sex life while married. He was the first man I'd trusted to reveal my forbidden fantasies to, in explicit, erotic detail. And oh, yeah, he was the first man I'd ever propositioned with an affair.

He'd agreed, and knowing that I was about to embark upon the hottest sexual adventure of my life, with a gorgeous, sexy man who promised to push me beyond those conventional vanilla boundaries, I couldn't wait to get started.

Jase insisted on putting my chocolate cake

and milk on his tab. After paying Mallory, he left a generous tip on the bar for the girl, then turned to me.

"You ready to head out, puma?" he teased, laughter crinkling the skin around his eyes.

"Oh, you're funny," I said sarcastically as I slid off my barstool, but I was smiling, too. "And yes, I'm ready to go."

I started for the exit, with Jase following behind. As soon as we were outside, he grabbed my hand without asking and laced our fingers together, much like he had back in the bar, but this time the gesture felt intimate and possessive. Like we were a couple, when we weren't. It was something I tried very hard not to think about, nor did I want to analyze the little twist of disappointment that thought evoked.

His palm was big and warm, his fingers long, and my hand felt engulfed in his. Protected. Safe. Secure. All the things that had no business being a part of this fling of ours. Yet I couldn't bring myself to sever the connection, because if I was honest with myself, it was a novel thing for me to feel protected, safe, and secure, and I liked it.

It was easier to recognize now that those sentiments had been missing in my marriage. Not the physical aspect of being protected but the emotional comfort of knowing, and believing, that a person had my back. That hadn't been the case with Drew, who'd been more focused on his own goals than on making sure that I had everything I'd needed emotionally. He'd taken advantage of my willingness to put my dreams on hold, to work sixty-plus hours a week with two different jobs, so he could pursue his aspirations of being a trauma surgeon, while leading me to assume he'd return the favor once our massive school loans were paid off.

I'd believed him. Trusted him. He'd given me a false sense of safety and security, then left me reeling with the realization that I'd wasted ten years of my life on a man who had very easily replaced me with another younger woman.

"Hey, you're awfully quiet," Jase said in a low, concerned tone as we reached my car. "Are you okay?"

I exhaled a deep breath and pushed those dismal thoughts out of my mind. For the next few weeks, or however long this thing between me and Jase lasted, it was going to be all about the two of us—seduction, desires, and pleasure.

I glanced up at him in the shadowed darkness of evening and smiled. "I'm great," I said, and meant it. "How about you?"

Letting go of my hand, he gently backed me up against the side of my vehicle, his hot, hard body pressing along the length of mine. "I'll be much better as soon as I kiss you like I've been dying to for the past two hours."

My lips automatically parted in invitation, and I placed my hands on the waistband of his jeans. *Oh, yes, please.*

Heat flickered in his gaze as he lifted a hand, slid his palm affectionately along my cheek, then tangled his fingers into my hair. He tightened his hold around the strands, giving him complete control of how he positioned my mouth beneath his.

Anticipation rushed through me as he made me wait for his kiss, deliberately letting the tension between us build while making sure that he was the one who decided when and how he was going to take my mouth. His eyes darkened, his expression reflecting a combination of escalating lust and need.

God, I loved him like this. In charge. A little forceful. And absolutely confident in his ability to give me pleasure. *Oh, yes, especially that.*

"Jase," I whispered, my tone breathless and pleading.

He finally angled my head to the side and gradually lowered his. I closed my eyes, expecting to feel the crush of his mouth, wanting that desperately. But instead he nibbled on my lower lip and used his tongue to skim across the plump flesh, so softly, so sensually I felt that slow, hot lick right between my thighs.

I shivered against him, whimpered in the back of my throat, and he finally sealed his lips over mine and deepened the kiss, sweeping my senses into overload as his tongue stroked and tangled with mine, and his mouth devoured and consumed. He took what he wanted, stealing my sanity right along with my modesty. I didn't care that we were outside in the open, that he had me pinned up against my vehicle. All I could think about was alleviating the growing, throbbing ache down below.

Moaning with the need for more pressure, more friction, I widened my stance and pulled on the waistband of his pants so his hips met mine, but the hem of my dress was a frustrating barrier between us. The solid length of his erection pushing against my mound was a grinding tease, and nowhere near where I ached for it the most.

He'd started a slow burn back in the bar, when he'd slipped his hand beneath my dress and rubbed my clit, then left me wanting. Now, the spiraling heat was escalating all over again. I could feel how wet I was, could feel the demanding pulse of my pussy, and I managed, just barely, to pull my mouth from his.

"Touch me, Jase," I said raggedly, brazenly. "Make me come. Here. Now."

He buried his face against the side of my neck, his breathing hot and damp against my skin. "Pull up your skirt," he ordered gruffly.

I did, quickly raising the hem until it was bunched up around my hips. He slid his free hand down the back of my thigh, hooked his fingers around my knee, and pulled my leg up to his hip so that the length of his erection was aligned right against my sex. It wasn't at all what I'd been expecting, but the firm pressure was exactly what my body craved.

I was still wearing my panties, but as he started to move against me, the rough denim of his jeans scraped the insides of my thighs, and the stiff bulge beneath the zippered fly rubbed against my clit. He kissed and bit my neck and sucked on a patch of skin as he pumped his hips faster, thrust harder, and the exquisite combination of textures and the rhythmic, accurate strokes had me climaxing very quickly.

I gripped his T-shirt in my fists as I jolted against him, my leg tightening around his hip as I fell over the peak and straight into infinite pleasure. A soft cry rose up in my throat, but before it could completely escape, his mouth was on mine again, buffering the sound with a deep, tongue-tangling kiss while my body shuddered hard against him.

When the orgasm finally ebbed, he released my leg, freed my mouth, and tucked my face against his neck to give me a moment to regain my bearings. The hand in my hair gently massaged my scalp; the other slid around my waist to hold me close and keep my shaking legs from collapsing. As the fog of desire cleared from my mind, my surroundings came back into focus, reminding me exactly where we were.

"I can't believe I let you do that to me in a public parking lot," I murmured incredulously against his throat.

He chuckled, the low, rumbling sound vibrating in his chest. "I can't, either," he said, his voice husky with humor. "But I made sure no one was around."

"At least one of us did," I mumbled, my face flushing with embarrassment when I thought about the provocative show I could have given someone.

He continued stroking my hair. "Ahh, I guess exhibitionism isn't another deep, dark fantasy you harbor?" he teased.

"No, not at all," I replied primly. "I'm very old-fashioned that way."

He laughed out loud and drew my head back to look into my eyes. "There is nothing old-fashioned about you when it comes to sex, and I like it that way."

He shifted against me, his shaft still firm and heavy between us, a tangible reminder that he was still fully aroused when he'd just given me an amazing orgasm. An overhead parking lot lamp a couple of vehicles away cast a glow of light across his gorgeous face, revealing the tense set to his jaw and the banked hunger and need in his eyes.

I slid a hand down the hard plane of his muscled chest, past the waistband of his jeans, and stroked my palm over his erection. I heard him inhale a sharp breath, and squeezed him just enough to add to the sensual torment. "Come home with me, Jase." Now that I was ready to be sexually adventurous, there was so much more I wanted to do with him and to him. And definitely not in public.

He groaned and pushed his hips against my hand, but his features were etched with regret as he shook his head. "As much as I'd like to go home with you, not tonight."

His words said one thing while his body said another. I gave him a sultry, coaxing smile. "I'm a sure thing, Jase," I said, knowing he'd remember the last time I'd said something similar to him, when I'd all but pushed him to go out with Nicole.

He laughed but didn't give in to my offer. "I have an early morning tomorrow."

"Oh." The rejection stung. I glanced away, suddenly feeling hesitant and too damn insecure. "I guess I should go then."

He stopped me when I tried to wriggle away from him, the big hands on my hips keeping me in place. "Kendall, look at me."

His voice was soft but firm, compelling me to do as he asked. I met his gaze and lifted my chin, trying hard not to let my stupid self-doubts show.

He must have seen the uncertainty on my face, because he swore beneath his breath. His own gaze softened as he brushed an errant strand of hair off my cheek, his touch so gentle and caring. "It's not that I don't want you. Don't *ever* think that, and especially not when you can feel for yourself how hard you make me. It's taking every bit of restraint that I have not to fuck you up against the side of your car until you scream my name."

I knew my eyes were wide, a bit shocked even. "Then why?"

He exhaled deeply. "So much has already happened tonight. With you and Grant. With you and me. And I don't want to throw sex into the mix of everything else. I want us to start fresh and both to be clear-headed the next time we're together. Just the two of us."

His reasoning made perfect sense and eased my mind. "Okay."

He skimmed the pad of his thumb along my jaw, his expression reflecting his relief that I understood. "All that being said, go out with me this weekend."

I blinked at him. "Go out with you?"

"Yeah," he said with a persuasive grin. "On a date."

I experienced a moment of panic. Our agreement back at the bar, *a fling*, hadn't included time together outside of the bedroom. "This affair isn't about *dating*." Dating implied a courtship, the start of an emotional relationship. All the things I knew I couldn't have with Jase, so why put myself in that kind of position?

He gave me a smile that was both adorable and unwavering. "If you want sex, then I want something in return. A date."

I arched a brow. "Quid pro quo?"

"Tit for tat," he replied with a shrug.

I laughed, even knowing that Jase was winning the debate. "That sounds dirty."

"I can make it as dirty as you want it to be," he promised with a flirtatious wink. "But before we get to the dirty stuff, I just want to spend a few hours with you with our clothes *on*. We'll go and do something fun during the day, and then I'm all yours for the night."

I bit my bottom lip, so very tempted by his suggestion. I knew it wasn't a smart idea to mix play with pleasure when it came to Jase, but it had been such a long time since I'd done anything for the sheer fun of it, or allowed myself to be carefree. Work and responsibilities were all I'd known for years, before and after my divorce. Didn't I deserve a day to indulge and enjoy whatever Jase planned?

Yes, I did, I decided, and embraced my decision.

"Okay, you win again," I told him, and didn't miss the triumphant smirk on his lips. "I work all day Saturday at the studio, but I do have Sunday off."

"Saturday isn't great for me, either. Mac and

I have an appointment with a consulting firm in L.A. to discuss improvements on their computer network and server efficiency, which will take most of the day," he said. "So Sunday is great for me, too."

"Then consider it a...date." Now that I was all in, I was anxious to see what the day would bring and what Jase considered fun.

Sunday night, however, he was all mine.

SATURDAY AT PURE BLISS passed quickly for me. With three boudoir sessions set up throughout the day, I'd been incredibly busy, and I'd booked four other appointments for later on in the week with new clients. With all the referrals and my rapidly growing business, I was considering hiring a front-end girl. Someone to answer phones and schedule appointments and greet customers as they arrived. Someone to help me tidy up the studio at the end of the day.

Handling all aspects of the business was becoming a bit overwhelming, and I was grateful that I was at a point where I could finally afford to bring in my first official employee. I'd worked damn hard to get to this point, and I was proud of my accomplishments and success and just how viable my company had become. Next week, I'd post the job position in the local paper and online and go from there.

My last appointment of the day was Stacie, the woman who'd come into the studio the previous week to view her boudoir photos and place her order for what she wanted. She was alone again and without the older gentleman who'd accompanied her to the initial photo session. I wasn't sure what their involvement was, since neither of them had put a label to their relationship, but the fact that they were adamant that their faces be concealed in the photographs I had taken made me curious about the couple. Then again, maybe they wanted to display the portraits in a more public way, without their identities being obvious to others.

The reasons didn't really matter, and they weren't any of my business. What my customers wanted, I gave them. What they did with the photos, or how they displayed the pictures, was up to them.

I quickly went to my office and picked up the glossy-handled bag with the platinum package that Stacie had ordered, which included a collection of enlarged photos that had been mounted and framed, another collection of standard-size prints, and the red leather-bound photo book filled with over two dozen provocative shots of the couple. Stacie was waiting in the sitting area where I met with clients to set up appointments and to deliver the photos they ordered, and I greeted the pretty, auburn-haired young woman with a smile.

"Hi, Stacie," I said as I walked into the room. "How are you today?"

"Just great." Stacie's light green eyes were filled with excitement as she watched me set the compilation of photos on the table in front of her. "I'm so anxious to take a look at the finished product. I'm seeing Richard tonight and can't wait to surprise him with the portraits and photo book."

"Well, here they are." I was always a little

nervous myself until I had my client's final approval. "I hope you like them."

Stacie perused all the pictures and flipped through the photo book, her expression delighted and thrilled with the final delivery. She turned a page in the leather-bound book and bit her bottom lip as she stared at one of the more suggestive images of her and Richard that I had taken on the cream-colored silk lounge chair in the studio—with Stacie on her back and Richard's head down between her thighs, his hands tugging away her panties. The younger woman's face was turned away from the camera, her body arched in passion, with one hand buried in her lover's hair. The lavender silk robe she'd worn had fallen off her shoulder, exposing the soft curve of her breast.

I remembered that shot—and just how into the moment the couple had been.

"He might be an older man, but damn, he's so freakin' hot," Stacie said, her full mouth curving into a sly smile. "I'm such a lucky girl."

I smiled and gave in to my curiosity. "Have you been dating long?"

Stacie thought for a moment as she viewed

another glossy photo. "We've been seeing each other for about a year now."

"Ahh, so it's serious."

"I'd like to think so." The other woman exhaled a small, disheartened sigh and held up her left hand, bare of any jewelry. "But until I have a ring on my finger, nothing is guaranteed, is it?"

"No, that's true," I agreed. Hell, even *with* a ring nothing was guaranteed, as I well knew.

"I just keep waiting for Richard…to get his shit together," Stacie said, suddenly sounding frustrated and irritated.

Sensing that whatever Stacie was *waiting on* was a big source of contention between the couple, I let the conversation go. I wrapped up the appointment within the next twenty minutes, and was relieved when Stacie expressed her full satisfaction over the photos.

Once the other woman was gone, I cleaned up, then shut down the studio, my mind drifting to Jase and our date tomorrow. I had to admit that I was excited to see him and curious to find out what he'd planned for the day. I was already filled with anticipation, like a young girl with my first boy crush. Except Jase was all man—every single inch of him.

But before I saw him tomorrow, I had one more important thing to do. After locking up Pure Bliss, I headed down the street to Raina's shop, Sugar and Spice, to purchase some sexy, risqué toys and pretty lingerie. If I was going to make the most of my affair with Jase, then I intended to shed all my sexual inhibitions and be as bad and naughty as I'd always secretly wanted to be.

CHAPTER 10

Jase

I headed up to the apartment number that Kendall had texted me last night and knocked on her door. She lived in a gated and guarded complex, which appeased the security guy in me. I liked knowing that she was safe and secure when I wasn't around.

Possessive much? Yeah, so I was a little—okay, a lot—protective of Kendall. She was a woman who could clearly take care of herself, but since the moment I'd met her a month ago, then learning about her shitty marriage, I'd felt the inexplicable urge to be the guy who gave her a sense of security and showed her through my actions that not all men treated women as badly as her ex had.

The more time I spent with Kendall, the more those attentive feelings grew. And as much as I knew that what she wanted out of life *now* didn't mesh with my own aspirations and timeline for marriage and kids, I couldn't bring myself to walk away from her, either. But right or wrong, I just wanted to enjoy my time with her, and hopefully at some point, we'd come to some kind of compromise in our relationship—even though we were at different points in our lives.

I shook my head of those discouraging thoughts, refusing to dwell on something that wasn't an issue right at this moment. All I could do was keep things in perspective, take things one day at a time, and today was all about having fun together—outside of the bedroom.

I lifted my hand to knock again just as the door flung open. Kendall stood there, breathless and smiling—and so completely, stunningly beautiful she made my heart trip in my chest. Her hair was in a high ponytail, and she was wearing minimal makeup, just mascara and gloss on her lips from what I could tell. She looked youthful and pretty and happy to see me, and witnessing how excited she was about today was exactly what I needed to see to make me fully relax.

"I'm so sorry," she said, pressing a hand to her chest, her cheeks pink from being so flustered. "I was finishing getting dressed when you first knocked and had to scramble to get the rest of my clothes on."

I smiled slowly, wickedly. "I would have been more than happy to come in and help."

She laughed and shook her head as she stepped back to let me into her apartment. "Somehow I think your idea of helping would have been more of a hindrance, and we'd probably end up spending the day inside instead of out."

"You're probably right," I admitted. I would have been stripping her out of her clothes rather than putting them over her sexy curves.

She gave me a chastising look that was more playful than stern. "You're such a bad boy," she said as she walked toward an adjoining room in her small apartment. "I just need to get a few things and I'll be ready to go."

She sashayed her way to what I assumed was the bedroom, and I watched her go, resisting the urge to follow her and strip her out of her clothes, anyway. Yeah, I *was* bad. Unapologetically so, when it came to her.

She disappeared from my view, and I pushed my hands into the front pockets of my khaki shorts and glanced around. Her place was small. Real small. Only a few steps inside the apartment and I was literally standing in a kitchenette with just enough room for a table that could seat two, which connected to a tiny living room with a couch and coffee table and a TV mounted on the wall. There wasn't room for anything more.

There were two other doors, one leading into a half bathroom and the other her bedroom. The place was sparsely decorated with a few framed pictures on the wall that looked as though she might have taken them herself. But everything else was just the bare minimum, and I wondered if it was by choice or because she'd had to start from scratch after her divorce. I had a feeling it was more the latter.

But despite that setback in her life, she'd clearly made her boudoir photography and studio a priority over living space. She'd learned to be economical during her marriage —a person didn't pay off two hundred thousand dollars in debt in ten years if they weren't exceptionally thrifty—and how to tightly budget and prioritize spending. It was a trait that I admired. Kendall was so much stronger and resilient, emotionally *and* mentally, than she probably realized.

A few minutes later, when she came back out carrying a large straw purse and wearing a pair of flip-flops, I realized I'd never seen her dressed so casually before. She had on white shorts that drew my gaze to her lean thighs and slender legs, and a light pink tank top—I was beginning to think pink was a favorite color of hers. Beneath the outfit I could see the outline of a bikini top and bottoms, which was exactly how I'd told her to dress, with the ability to strip off the outer layer and be beach-ready in seconds.

"Okay, I think I'm good," she said as she started for the door.

I gently caught her arm as she passed by, bringing her to a sudden stop, and she looked up at me with wide, startled eyes.

"I think you forgot something," I said, and stroked my thumb along the soft, sensitive flesh of her inner arm.

She frowned, as if mentally reviewing the list of items she had in her head that she needed to take with her today. "What did I forget?"

"To kiss me," I murmured, then waited to see what she would do, because the sexy part of this date was all on her.

She didn't disappoint me. With a sultry smile, she closed the distance between us, skimmed her hands along the T-shirt covering my chest, and looped her arms around my neck. She lifted up on the tips of her toes, pressing her body even closer, and brushed her lips across mine with a soft sigh I felt all the way down to my groin.

I slid my hands around her waist, then lower, so I could grab and knead her delectable ass with my fingers and grind my hips against hers. I groaned when she lightly bit my bottom lip, then soothed the sting with a slow, sensual slide of her tongue.

I waited, not so patiently, for her to deepen the kiss while heat and anticipation thrummed through my veins. But she kept things sweet and chaste, her lips a soft, teasing promise that made me want to bury my hands in her hair and take complete control of the kiss. And her.

It took extreme effort to let her play this particular game her way, and when she finally finished tormenting me and eased away from my body, I reluctantly let her go. I met her gaze, and she licked her lips as if to taste me. Her eyes sparkled mischievously, shamelessly, and damn if all that confidence didn't turn me on, too.

I set my hands on my hips and arched a brow, though I was gratified to see the rise and fall of her chest, as well as her nipples poking against her tank top, proof that she was just as aroused as I was. "So that's how it's going to be today?"

She blinked at me, much too innocently. "What way?"

I exhaled a breath, which did nothing to

ease the pressure of my stiff cock. "A long, slow tease until tonight."

"It's called sexual tension," she said, her ponytail bouncing sassily as she headed back toward the door. "Think you can resist me until we get back later this evening?"

I grinned and followed her out of the apartment, making sure the door was locked behind me. "I'm going to try my hardest, but I make no guarantees." I had a feeling she was going to make sure it was a long, *hard* day. Hard being the operative word.

Taking my sunglasses from where they were perched on the top of my head, I slipped them on as I escorted her out to the parking area and toward our ride for the day. When I pointed my remote toward a black Audi R8 Spyder convertible and the sports car chirped as I disengaged the alarm, her jaw nearly dropped.

"I thought you drove a truck," she said, glancing at me incredulously. "Dean must be paying you extremely well over at Noble and Associates for you to afford this car, too."

"I *wish* it were mine." I grinned as I opened the passenger-side door for her. "Don't get too excited. It's only ours for the day. It has to be returned to the rental place by tomorrow."

She slid very carefully into the soft leather seat, holding her straw bag close to her chest as if she was afraid it would scratch something. "The car even *smells* like money. It must have cost you a small fortune, even for a day."

I closed her door and walked around the hood of the vehicle to the driver's side and got inside. "Actually, the owner of the luxury car rental place is a client of Noble and Associates. I did some cyber security work for them a few months ago, and the guy gave me a discount too good to pass up. It's all about impressing the girl, and my truck just wasn't going to cut it today," I said with a wink.

She set her purse down on the floorboard between her feet and buckled in. "I really hate to admit it, but I'm suitably impressed. This car is just…wow."

I turned the key in the ignition, and the car started with a smooth but powerful rumble that made me grin like a teenage boy.

She laughed. "Oh, my God, this car is just as much for *you* as it is to impress me."

I couldn't lie as I revved the engine. "Yeah, maybe a little."

After leaving her apartment complex, I drove toward Pacific Beach in La Jolla. Most women would have asked where we were going, but Kendall didn't seem to care and just enjoyed the ride in the convertible, with the wind whipping through her ponytail, the sun on her face, and a delighted smile on her lips.

Once we arrived at our destination, we stripped down to our swimsuits to play in the ocean, then relaxed on the beach on the large towels I had brought with us. I rented bikes for us to ride along the boardwalk, where we stopped and walked through some of the shops while holding hands, and had a late lunch/early dinner at an outdoor cafe. We drove a little farther along the scenic route and watched as the sun set in the Pacific, framed by the sculptural sandstone cliffs in Ocean Beach.

The entire day was all about fun and play. Laughter and flirting and light, easy, getting-to-know-more-about-you conversation—along with a few stolen kisses that reminded us both how the evening would end. There was no thinking or worrying or discussing anything serious. I deliberately took us both out of our normal element to someplace where we could just unwind and enjoy each other's company, no pressure or expectations. By the time we returned back to Kendall's place, we were so in sync and comfortable with each other it felt as though we'd been dating for months, instead of just the one day.

I want this with her, I thought as she set her straw purse down on the small table in the kitchenette, then turned around to face me, her eyes bright, her expression content. I wanted this comfortable, easy relationship that included dating and being together beyond sex and spending time with one another just because we were building an underlying friendship to complement and strengthen the attraction and intimacy we'd already established.

Everything about the two of us felt perfect and so damn right, and today was proof that it wasn't just about the sex, or an unemotional affair, not when we connected on so many other levels beyond physical.

She walked toward me, now only wearing her bikini top and shorts. I'd brought sunscreen with us, and we'd both used it, but her cheeks were a light, healthy shade of pink, as were the tops of her shoulders. When she was close enough to touch, I gently ran the tip of my finger down her nose and smiled at her.

"I think I see…freckles," I said, tracing a few of the light brown dots on her face, then across her shoulder.

Her mouth quirked adorably. "Yeah, the sun tends to bring them out. I hated them as a kid. Can't say I love them as an adult, either."

"I like them. You even have a few on your chest," I mused, and used the opportunity to skim my finger along the inner edges of her bikini top and along the soft curve of her breasts in her cleavage.

Her nipples puckered tightly, and just when I would have untied those bikini strings to get a better look at those freckles, she took a step back and shook her head. "First, I need to take a shower. I feel sandy in inappropriate places," she said humorously. "You can take one after me."

So much for getting an invite to join her, I thought in disappointment, but let her do things her way. For now. We both knew exactly where this evening was heading and how it would end, and there was no reason to rush what I wanted to last for hours.

I stripped off my T-shirt and waited in the small kitchenette while drinking a cold bottle of water. Twenty long minutes later, she walked out of her bedroom, tying the sash on a cream-colored silk robe. Her hair looked as though it had been washed and quickly dried. It was now piled high on her head in a messy knot my fingers itched to take down so I could wrap those soft strands tightly around my fists to make her do dirty things to me and my stiffening cock. There was no way I was allowing her to deprive me of that pleasure—I'd take her hair down myself if I had to.

"Your turn," she said, glancing up at me with a smile. "While you're in the shower, I can get ready."

"Ready?" Hell, I was ready to get down and dirty right now.

Her lashes fell half-mast as she skimmed a finger down the center of my chest. "To seduce you."

The muscles in my abdomen flexed when she reached my navel, then ventured down to the waistband of my shorts. A little lower and she'd have her hands full of thick, hard cock. "Sweetheart, I was seduced the moment I saw you this morning."

Something warm and sweet flickered in her gaze at my admission, as if she enjoyed knowing she had the ability to beguile me "I'm *upping* the seduction ante. Now go."

After that promise, she didn't have to tell me twice, because I was curious as hell to find out what she had planned. I headed into the bathroom, took a lukewarm shower, and ignored the fact that the rigid length of my dick was waiting for a hand job to ease some of the pressure in my balls.

Nope. Wasn't going to happen. I was saving every single solid inch for her, I thought with a smirk.

I scrubbed my body with her liquid soap that smelled like vanilla because there wasn't any other option, and washed my hair. I ran a hand over the light stubble on my face, opting not to use her razor to shave, because I wanted her to feel the soft scratch of my whiskers between her thighs. Once I was done, I shut off the water, grabbed the soft, fluffy towel she'd left out for me, and rubbed it through my hair and dried my body.

Since I figured I was going to be naked fairly soon, I wrapped the towel around my waist and tucked the end into a knot to keep it secure, unable to hide the way my erection made a tent in the fabric. A quick comb of my hands through my damp hair and I was good to go.

I opened the door and walked out of the bathroom and directly into her bedroom. Two steps in and I jerked to a stop when my gaze found Kendall standing by the foot of the bed, completely transformed into a stunningly gorgeous, exceptionally sexy, delectable woman. A vixen. A temptress. A siren brought to life to fulfill all my filthy fantasies.

I'd left her in a silk robe, but now she wearing a tight-fitting, peach-hued cropped camisole top made of see-through lace. The stretchy fabric fit her body like a second skin, molding to her perky breasts and teasing me with a glimpse of her dusky aureoles and the darker pink nub of her stiff nipples jutting against the sheer lace. My gaze slid lower, taking in the tiny matching lace panties, the thigh-high pale cream stockings, and the bewitching high heels that screamed for me to wrap those inviting legs around my waist so I could feel the spiked heel dig into my back as I plowed into her.

I clenched my jaw, trying my best to ignore the fierce erection straining against the front of my towel as I slowly, deliberately dragged my gaze back up to her face—now framed by her disheveled, wavy hair that she'd taken down. I was surprised by the hint of uncertainty flickering in her eyes and the way she shifted nervously on those provocative heels, as if she was anxiously awaiting my approval.

I didn't hesitate to give it to her. "*Fuck me,*" I murmured, those raw words of praise seemingly chasing away any of her lingering doubts.

"Oh, I plan to," she said huskily, that sassy side of her finally coming out to play.

I chuckled as I made my way closer. She was feisty tonight, and I could see her growing more and more confident in herself as I approached. Oh, yeah, I wanted her bold and brazen and uninhibited in every way.

My gaze skimmed past her to the pink-handled bag on the end of the bed. Stopping beside her, I tipped my head questioningly. "What's in the bag?" It hadn't been there when I'd gone into the bathroom.

She drew her bottom lip between her teeth, then lifted her chin a few notches, as if she'd just given herself a mental boost of courage. "It's filled with sexy toys I want to try. I bought them at Raina's store."

A part of me was shocked that she'd gone out in public to purchase erotic toys to increase our pleasure, and the other part was seriously elated and turned on that she wanted to elevate our sex play. "Show me what dirty things you want me to do to you."

"It's not *all* about me," she amended playfully. "There's a few naughty things I want to do to *you*, too."

She grabbed the paper bag and dumped the contents on the bed, and out tumbled a variety of interesting and arousing items: a G-spot stimulator, nipple clamps, restraints, anal toys, lubrication, condoms, and oh, damn...

I glanced at her incredulously. "You bought a vibrating cock ring?"

Her eyes danced with laughter. "At least I didn't buy the cock *cage*."

Jesus. I knew exactly what a cock cage was—a male version of a chastity belt that made an erection extremely uncomfortable—and I winced at the thought of my member being confined in that torture device. "No…just no."

"I agree, which is why I went with the cock ring," she said, much too amused by my reaction to the other gadget. "Raina said that it will keep you harder longer, with the added bonus of this vibrator for my pleasure." Expression intrigued, she picked up the package and examined the silver item on the ring that looked like a small bullet and would vibrate against her clit when I was inside of her.

"Keeping it up isn't an issue for me." I indicated my current state of arousal, still confined by the towel. "But I'll have to thank Raina for her input on the cock ring," I said derisively, just as another thought occurred to me. "I hope you don't plan on using all these things tonight." I had stamina, but every man had an *I'm fucking drained and can't get it up again* point, and considering the things *I* wanted to do to her tonight, she needed to pace herself with the toys.

"Yeah, that would be a bit much," she

agreed. "I figure we have time to try them all over the next few weeks."

I was relieved, yet I hated the reminder of our limited time together.

Kicking the thought from my mind, I focused on Kendall and right now, instead. "Which toy do you want to try first?"

"Mmm." She considered her purchases, then finally picked up one of the packages, her eyes glimmering with anticipation. "This G-spot stimulator. I couldn't tell you where mine is, and I'm curious to know what it feels like."

I could easily show her with the crook of my finger rubbing just inside her inner walls but decided that the toy would be way more fun. "Okay, the G-spot stimulator it is."

While I opened the box to retrieve the device, she put the rest of the items back in the bag, though she left the condoms on the night-stand for us to use. I sat down on the side of the bed and kept my towel intact for now.

"Come here," I said, pointing to the spot between my knees.

She positioned herself in front of me so that my legs bracketed her thighs and my face was level with her chest. Tipping my head back, I glanced up at her with a smile while caressing my hands up the backs of her thighs. "I love these panties," I said, tracing a finger along the waistband of the light orange lace fabric. "Especially the color. Know what they remind me of?"

She shook her head, causing those loose waves to brush across her shoulders, which in turn made her nipples pebble even harder against her lace camisole. "No."

"The color reminds me of the way you taste right here," I murmured as I pressed two fingers along the front panel, and even through the material I could feel the soft folds of her sex and the dampness that was already seeping through. "Like sweet peach nectar. I can't wait to have your soft, delicious pussy in my mouth again."

She shivered and braced one of her hands on my shoulder, as if she needed to hold on to something solid to keep her steady. I had a feeling her legs were going to need a whole lot more support before I was done with her.

I kept my gaze pinned on hers as I grabbed the sides of her underwear and slowly inched them down her hips. "But as much as I love them, they're in my way, so off they go." I pushed the panties the rest of the way off and helped her step out of them so they didn't hinder the way I needed her to stand.

I could smell her arousal, could see that pink flesh beckoning to me, and it took every ounce of control I possessed not to drop down in front of her and bury my face between her thighs. Eventually, I'd get there, but right now, this was all about introducing her to a whole different sphere of pleasure.

"Spread your feet apart," I ordered, loving how she didn't hesitate to do as I asked. I picked up the smooth, slightly curved vibrator designed specifically to hit a woman's most sensitive spot and lightly skimmed the device up the inside of her thigh until the tip touched her clit. I hadn't even turned on the stimulator yet, or inserted it into her, and she was already breathing hard and quivering in anticipation.

Smiling to myself, I continued to tease the outer folds of her sex with the cool, sleek wand, then slid my free hand around her waist to draw her closer, to keep her body right where I wanted it so I could slide my tongue over her tight nipple through the rough texture of lace. She moaned, and the hand on my shoulder drifted to the back of my head to keep my mouth on her breast. Since she'd purchased nipple clamps, I gave her a hint of what to expect and used my teeth to nip and tug and bite that firm bead of flesh. She gasped at the sting of pain but didn't pull my mouth away. Instead, her back arched to encourage me to take more, and I did, sucking her flesh deep and strong.

She moved restlessly against my hand between her legs, her hips rocking and undulating, and I slid the toy inside of her, letting her adjust to the thick object before taking things up a notch. She made a soft, mewling sound of need, and with the stimulator pressed against her inner wall, I tightened my arm around her waist, then flipped the switch and turned the vibrator on.

She cried out in shock, and it only took a couple of strokes against that sensitive patch of skin inside her vagina to make her scream as she soared over the edge. Her head rolled back, and her entire body shook and writhed with the force of her orgasm. I felt her legs start to give out on her and knew she wouldn't be standing much longer. I removed the toy, and in the next instant, her knees buckled and her body went limp, and I had no choice but to gently guide her down so that she was kneeling on the floor and her head was resting on my thigh.

I stroked her hair, giving her as much time as she needed as her breathing slowed and she gradually recovered from her explosive climax. Many minutes later, she lifted her head, her face flushed and her gaze dreamy as she looked up at me from her position on the floor.

"This is me, worshipping you at your feet," she said, a touch of humor in her voice. "Because that was freakin' amazing and unlike any orgasm I've ever had before. I can still feel it fluttering inside me."

I chuckled, relieved that she was okay and had enjoyed the experience. And now that she was coming around and regaining her strength, I gave her a sinful smile. "I like you on your knees in front of me."

A renewed spark of desire gleamed in her pretty green eyes as her gaze shifted to the obvious erection straining beneath the towel still wrapped around my waist. "I suppose, while I'm down here, I should take care of this *big* problem you seem to have," she teased as she sat up, pushed my legs wider apart, then moved in between before tugging the knotted end of the towel so it came undone. She let the sides fall away, then licked her lips hungrily as she stared at my erection.

A shaft of heated lust surged through me as I waited impatiently, *desperately*, for her to touch me for the first time. I didn't even realize I was holding my breath until she wrapped her hand around me and I finally exhaled in relief —which was short-lived—as she gripped my length, glided her fingers up to the swollen, sensitive head, and used her thumb to smear the pre-come over the tip.

My hips jerked to instinctively pump my cock through her fist, and I swore beneath my breath while she looked up at me in pure delight, as if she liked having that bit of control over my pleasure.

"Will you…" Her voice trailed off, and she glanced away uncertainly.

"Tell me," I said, my voice a low demand. No way was she not finishing that sentence. "Tell me what you want, and I'll give it to you."

Her gaze came back to mine, that beautiful, brazen part of her emerging once again. "I want you to slide your hand in my hair and wrap the strands tight around your fingers," she said huskily. "I like the way it feels, that slight sting against my scalp when you pull. It's like being...restrained."

Oh, fuck. The honesty in those words nearly unraveled me. The fact that she liked it a little rough and forceful, *had asked for it that way*, set my blood on fire. I gathered her hair in my hand, twisting it relentlessly around my fist until her lips parted on a soft, silky moan of pleasure, her eyes glazed over with lust. With her movements under my command, I tugged her forward, aligned the tip of my cock against the damp heat of her mouth, and gently but firmly pressed her head down, so she had no choice but to take whatever I gave her.

Her lashes fluttered closed, and a silky purr of sound vibrated through her as she worked the underside of my shaft with her tongue as I slid even deeper, until every bit of my dick disappeared and I was pushing against her tight, constricting throat. I had to grit my teeth against the instinctive urge to jerk my hips upward. With immense restraint, I slowly guided her head back up to the crest and couldn't contain the fierce hiss of pleasure that escaped me at the mind-blowing feel of her hungry lips dragging up the length of my erection and the wet, greedy suction of her mouth caressing every single hard inch.

She smiled. I felt the satisfied curve of her lips against my cock right before I filled her back up again and began fucking her mouth, while she skimmed her hands down my chest and her fingernails scraped across my abdomen. The dual pleasure was so incredible, so intense, my entire body shuddered and my eyes rolled back in my head. I could only handle a few more strokes before the need expanding in my belly threatened to erupt. I was so goddamn close, but this wasn't how I intended to come.

I pulled her mouth off of my cock while I still had the willpower to do so, and she stared up at me from where she was kneeling between my legs, her eyes unfocused and dilated with desire and her lips wet and swollen from sucking me so eagerly.

"Not like this," I said gruffly, and grinned

incorrigibly. "If your mouth is going to be on my cock, then you know what I want, don't you?"

She understood and nodded jerkily. "You want your tongue on me at the same time," she said huskily, her eyes gleaming with a secret kind of thrill.

So prim and proper with her reply, when I wanted the dirty version. I gripped her hair tighter in my hand, until she moaned softly from the edge of pain I inflicted, and brought my face closer to hers. "Where, *exactly*, do I want my tongue, sweetheart?"

Her lips parted on a soft, aroused exhale. "On my pussy."

Fuck, yeah. "On your pussy *and* deep inside it."

I released her just long enough to position myself on her bed and tucked a few of her pillows behind my neck for comfort and leverage. She stood up and I motioned her over. "Come up here and straddle my mouth."

Her gaze darkened with a touch of excitement and a whole lot of desire. Tentatively, she arranged her gorgeous legs on either side of my head and lowered herself over my body so that she was facing my feet and had direct access to my cock. She was spread open like a feast right above me, her folds so delicate and pouty and slick with arousal, and I didn't hesitate to lick her sweet, decadent pussy—soft and slow, from her clit to her opening.

She tossed her head back and whimpered and shuddered, and it wasn't enough for me that it was just her hand stroking my shaft when I wanted the wet heat of her mouth again. I slid my hands around to her bare ass and smacked my palm against her bottom, hard enough to sting and get her attention. She gasped in surprise, and I rubbed my prickly cheek against the inside of her thigh, deliberately abrading her skin with my facial stubble so she'd have marks there tomorrow.

"Suck my cock, Kendall," I demanded gruffly as I flicked my tongue across her clit to heighten her arousal. "Unless you want another swat."

She made an inarticulate noise that could have been a curse or a plea, and she quickly obeyed my order. Her soft lips enveloped me completely, sliding all the way down to the base, then back up in a slow, wet suction that had my balls drawing up tight and sensation building deep in my core.

So fucking good. While she worked me over, I continued my own assault. I pushed two fingers inside of her and drew her clit into my mouth, rolling it around on my tongue until she moaned around my cock. I added a bit of pressure and friction and deepened my intimate, open-mouthed kiss on her cunt. I felt her body clench around my pumping fingers and knew by the mewling sounds she made and the way she was rocking against my mouth that she was approaching her orgasm. My own climax rose right along with hers, the tingling at the base of my spine, the pulse of lust surging along the length of my cock, against her tongue…

She wrenched her mouth from my shaft on a whimper, stunting my release in her quest to chase her own. I immediately withdrew my fingers from her pussy, refusing to give her what she wanted, what she needed, until she did the same with me.

"Jase." Her voice was laced with disappointment and frustration.

I understood, since she'd left me in the

same sorry state. With my free hand, I slapped her other ass cheek, feeling the burn against my own palm as she sucked in a sharp, quivering breath. "Do *not* stop sucking my cock," I said in a darkly aggressive tone. "You don't come until I do. At the same time. Do you understand?"

She was so on edge her thighs trembled, and I felt the brush of her hair on my abdomen as she nodded her acquiescence. Then her lips closed over the head of my cock as she went back down on me, deeply, eagerly.

I did the same for her, building the tension all over again but keeping the intense pleasure just out of her reach until I was ready to come, which didn't take long considering how enthusiastically she sucked me, how she took me all the way and swallowed around me. I grew thicker, harder, and I used my entire mouth to emulate the same rhythm as hers—stroking and licking every inch of her flesh until she was writhing on top of me with the need to climax. Overwhelming desire consumed me, and I surged my hips upward one last time as I came on a harsh groan—thick, hot, and pulsing against the back of her throat.

I fucked her with my fingers, slid my tongue over and around her clit, and kept my mouth against her pussy as those internal tremors of hers rolled into deep, contracting shudders as she came at the same time.

Moments later she fell onto her back on the bed next to me, both of us so weak and spent that neither one of us could move right away.

"Oh, my God," she finally breathed after a few minutes had passed. "I can't believe that I... that *we* did that."

I managed to roll to my side with a grunt, then crawled around so that I was at the foot of the bed where Kendall's head was. I looked down at her face, loving the soft, serene look in her eyes, the gorgeous flush on her skin, the way her hair was tousled around her head from my fingers, and especially the pink, puffy lips that had just thoroughly sucked my cock dry.

Damn, she looked sexy as fuck.

"You are such a dirty girl," I murmured with a grin.

She lifted a hand to the stubble on my cheek and sighed. "I never used to be."

I didn't want to analyze why that made me so happy, that I'd been the one to coax that naughty part of her personality out to play. And damn if it didn't make me jealous at the thought of any other man knowing this incredibly passionate side to Kendall when I didn't want to share her with anyone.

Grabbing her hand, I kissed her fingertips, trying to keep my perspective about our relationship in place. "I'm so glad you're a dirty girl with me."

"Me, too," she whispered, a playful smile on her lips.

"That's a good thing, because we're not even close to being done tonight," I said as I waggled my brows with wicked intent. "And the next thing I plan to do to you is absolutely fucking filthy."

Her eyes widened as I moved over her, even as she laughed breathlessly. "I can't wait to find out how filthy you can get."

CHAPTER 11

Kendall

The unfamiliar musical sound of a phone alarm pulled me out of a deep sleep, and I cracked my eyes open with a confused frown. It took me a moment to realize that the wake-up tune wasn't mine but belonged to Jase's cell phone. He'd been cuddled up behind me for most of the night, and he rolled toward the nightstand on the other side of the bed to shut off the annoying sound.

"Good morning, sweetheart," he said softly, even a bit cajolingly.

"What time is it?" I asked in a raspy voice as I squinted at the bedroom window. It was still dark out, and the sun hadn't even started rising yet. Normally, I didn't get up until eight since I didn't have to be in the studio until ten, and I realized I was a grumpy morning person if someone—in this case, Jase—woke me up before the crack of dawn. I'd gotten used to my own schedule, my own routine, and this new adjustment was jarring.

"It's five o'clock," he said as he moved up behind me again beneath the covers, sounding much too cognizant considering his annoying phone had just disturbed the both of us from a satisfying, restful slumber.

"Why so early?" I complained as I buried my face into my pillow.

"It's Monday," he said, his tone amused. "I hit the gym at six every morning before work during the week. So I need to go pretty soon."

I made a sound of disgust. "That's two strikes against you. Being so chipper before the sun even rises and having a strict workout regimen you actually stick to."

His easy, masculine laughter drifted up to my ears. "Not much of a morning person, huh?"

A petulant grunt was my only response, which pretty much confirmed his question. Not that I cared. I was exhausted this morning, my muscles aching in places they never had before from all the various sex positions we'd tried and the different toys we'd played with. Those nipple clamps—while fun and pleasurable at the time when Jase had used them on me while I'd been restrained to my own bed— had left my breasts tender once he'd removed them. Even now the tips throbbed, and they probably would for the rest of the day.

Not to mention how many times he'd spanked my ass or the way he'd chafed the insides of my legs with his stubble. The rogue.

His lips touched down on the curve of my shoulder in a warm kiss, and just like sleeping beauty, my body started to stir to life, damn him. I squeezed my eyes shut, determined to ignore him, but the man didn't play fair and was now acquainted with too many of my physical and sexual weaknesses. Which was pretty much everything when it came to him.

I wasn't wearing anything at all, neither was Jase, and he trailed his fingers lightly down my side, along the indent of my waist, over the rise of my hip, then back up again, awakening all my feminine senses. My sensitive nipples tightened, and even though I would have sworn that I didn't have an orgasm left in me after all the ones he'd wrung out of me the night before, the tingling between my thighs begged to differ.

"I hate early mornings," I grumbled, trying to resist him and knowing it was a losing battle. But I didn't want to make it easy on him, either.

"Maybe I can change your mind about that," he murmured as he kissed my neck, causing goose bumps to rise on my skin.

Desire swirled in my belly, spilling downward between my legs. "Doubt it," I said, even knowing I was issuing a challenge to a man who loved a good dare and wouldn't hesitate to follow through on his promise. *At least that's what I'm counting on*, I thought with a veiled smile.

"Hmm." His hand came up to my breast, gently kneading the soft flesh in his palm until my nipple was stiff, and I had to bite my bottom lip to stifle my moan of pleasure. "I think you're seriously miscalculating my power of persuasion."

His body was aligned along my backside, his erection nudging persistently against my bottom. "Don't you need to go so you don't miss your workout?" I teased.

He chuckled as he gently bit my neck, drawing an unexpected gasp from me. "This is my warm-up exercise," he said, then pressed his lips to my ear and destroyed the rest of my flirtatious resistance with his next words. "I'm not leaving until I fuck you one more time. How do you want it this time, sweetheart?"

Even though last night was supposed to be *my* seduction, Jase had pretty much been in control of how and when he'd taken me. The man hadn't lacked for creativity, especially with all my new toys, but I liked that he was giving me a choice this morning—though I was certain the sexual position I chose was all he'd allow me to dictate, and he'd take charge from there.

The thought had my heart racing with anticipation. "I want you to fuck me like this, from behind." It was my favorite position with him, because I secretly loved how he pinned my body in a way that felt as though he was dominating me, which forced me to succumb to the mindless bliss of just letting go with him.

I heard him tear open a condom and put it on, then fully expected him to push me onto my stomach, but he surprised me once again.

"Stay just like this, on your side," he said from behind me, and guided my top leg forward on the bed so that it was bent and my thighs were separated and open for him. His hand slid down over my bottom, his fingers following the crease of my ass until they glided through my slit.

"You're still so fucking wet," he said, exhaling a harsh breath against my hair as he lightly skimmed a finger over my clit. "Are you sore?"

"A little," I said, and moaned as he traced the folds of my sex, his expert touch making me wetter, more aroused. "Definitely in a good way, though I'm pretty sure you left beard burn on my thighs."

He chuckled, the sexy, masculine sound rippling down my spine like a sensual caress. "Yeah, I did," he admitted shamelessly as he pushed the tip of his cock against my opening. "I like you sore. Your breasts, between your legs, your pussy tingling with satisfaction. Every time your aching nipples rub against your bra or you sit down on your smarting ass, I want you to think about me and all the things I'm going to do to you tonight."

He gripped my hip in one hand, drawing my bottom closer as he slid all the way inside of me while using his own leg to keep mine apart. The angle was deliciously different and definitely gave him all the power over how hard and how deep he fucked me.

Right now, his thrusts were slow and lazy, and the fingers on my hip drifted back up to fondle my breasts and toy with my nipples while his other hand curled gently around my throat. He tipped my head back against his chest, which forced my back to arch and caused my ass to lift higher against his groin so his next stroke hit impossibly, endlessly deep.

I moaned, the sensation of being helpless, with my body his to command completely, heightening my need to stunning proportions. I would never consider myself submissive, but here in the bedroom, I loved being ruled and overwhelmed by Jase, loved the erotic thrill it gave me knowing he'd use my surrender in the most pleasurable way possible, for the both of us. And right now, with him driving into me so ruthlessly, his cock so thick and hot and hard, I knew my orgasm, when he allowed it, would be epic.

His hand left my breast and dropped between my thighs, his fingers going directly for my clit. He strummed that tight knot of flesh until I was panting, gasping, and begging for release.

"You ready to come?" he rasped, clearly on edge himself.

"Yes," I groaned wildly. "Oh, God, *yes!*"

His fingers swirled over my clit, his hips pistoned violently against mine, and with a feral, demanding growl, he sank his teeth into the tendons where my neck met my shoulder. The sharp bite of pain was so lustful, so possessive, it shocked through my entire system and sent a rush of white-hot sensation straight down to where we were joined.

I cried out as the tight pulse of my inner muscles milked his cock, and he slammed into me one last time, his body shuddering hard against mine from behind, his shaft tunneling so deep it stole my breath and left me reeling in the aftershocks of my orgasm.

"Jesus," Jase muttered as he flipped onto his back beside me, his chest heaving from exertion. "What a great way to start the day."

I agreed with a soft, "Mmm." Now that I was wide-awake, I lifted my arms over my head, stretched my body, and flexed my toes. Extending my limbs felt good, though a few of my muscles protested the action. "Wow, that gave my abdomen a workout. At least my exercise is done for the day."

He laughed as he turned his head toward me, his brows waggling devilishly as his gaze skimmed down my naked body. "Until tonight, when we give your legs and thighs a workout while you're riding my cock."

"I can't think of a better way to burn calories." I smiled, surprisingly comfortable in my nudity around Jase. Then again, he was a visual, sexual guy, and hiding any part of my body wasn't an option with him. He wouldn't allow it.

"I'm going to take a shower before I head out to the gym," he said as he moved off the bed. "As much as I like smelling like you and sex, it'll distract the hell out of me while I'm pumping iron, and I don't think the guys will appreciate me working out with a hard-on."

I laughed, though I liked the idea of being a distraction for him, because he'd no doubt be on my mind all day, as well. I watched him cross to the bathroom, enjoying the view of his firm ass as he walked away. He left the door open as he got into the shower, enabling me to go in and brush my hair and teeth after I slipped on my robe.

Back out in the bedroom, I took in the messy bed and the few toys we'd used that were still on the nightstand. I'd clean those and put them away after he was gone. I picked up the condom wrappers, my mouth quirking at the realization that we'd used five out of the dozen that I'd purchased. Nope, stamina hadn't been an issue for Jase at all. He was young and virile and energetic, and I'd never been so sexually satisfied in my entire life.

Even as I went out to the kitchen to make a cup of coffee, I couldn't stop thinking about my day with Jase yesterday. Our date, and what a great time I'd had with him. Everything about him was so comfortable and easy, from talking about our pasts and families to enjoying the same outdoor activities—the beach and bike riding and just strolling on the boardwalk hand in hand. When had I ever had such a perfect day with a guy? Quite possibly never.

I brewed a single cup, added some French vanilla creamer, and leaned against the counter as I sipped my much-needed caffeine. Yesterday afternoon had been fun and flirty, but last night, and this morning, had been spectacular. And when he'd fallen asleep in my bed and I'd woken up with him cuddled behind me, surprisingly there'd been no panic or alarm that he'd spent the entire night with me.

In fact, if I was honest with myself, I liked having Jase in my bed, and it came back to the way he made me feel safe and secure, which was something I could too easily get used to if I wasn't careful. I knew where the two of us stood in this fling, and I didn't want my needs for the future to get wrapped up in the present with Jase.

At his age, and as he was just starting his career with Noble and Associates, we were clearly on two vastly different paths, and I knew better than to think or believe that Jase was ready to settle down and be a family man. Hell, he'd pretty much told me he wasn't ready for any of those things that night at The Players Club, and I'd do well to remember that, beyond this affair, we were at opposite ends of the spectrum when it came to the direction of our lives.

I wrapped my hands around the warm mug and took a sip of the coffee. So, for now, the sex was good. Phenomenal. I was a modern woman who could appreciate and enjoy a hot tryst with a younger guy. Women had affairs all the time and kept their emotions intact, and so could I. And before Jase grew bored of me like my husband had, I'd end things so we could go our separate ways.

We both knew it was inevitable. We'd agreed to the affair to sate our attraction to one another, nothing more. But deep in my heart, after spending the day with him yesterday, it *felt* like more, and yeah, that knowledge scared me because falling for Jase would be too complicated and heartbreaking.

"Hey, you look awfully serious when you

should be grinning from ear to ear after that great morning sex we had."

I managed a smile as I watched Jase walk into my tiny kitchen, wearing his shorts and T-shirt from the day before, his hair damp from his shower. He looked gorgeous, a little too cocky, and oh-so-confident in his ability to seduce me all over again. Which I knew he easily could. The man was walking sex on two legs and had an impressive package to go with it.

"Just trying to *really* wake up with a shot of caffeine," I said, lifting the mug for him to see. "Want a cup of coffee before you go?"

He shook his head as he stopped directly in front of me. "Not before I work out." Very slowly, he lifted his hand and tucked a stray strand of hair behind my ear, his gaze on mine. "Thank you," he said softly.

I got the impression he wasn't expressing his gratitude for my offer of coffee. His eyes were dark and serious, and something deep in my chest fluttered nervously. "For?" I prompted.

"Just being you," he said, his words simple, yet his tone was low and intimate. "Sweet.

Kind. Generous. Those qualities are hard to find in a woman. Or at least they have been for me."

His comment was so unexpected a lump rose in my throat. I didn't know what to say to that, and he spoke again before I could come up with a response.

A small smile kicked up the sides of his mouth. "And thank you for giving me, and us, a chance."

I set my coffee cup on the counter, the panic I hadn't experienced earlier now rushing to the surface. "Jase, this…*affair* doesn't change anything between us." We both *knew* that.

He squeezed his eyes shut as if he were in some kind of pain, then opened them again. "Jesus, I want it to. So bad."

His words caused something deep in my chest to hurt and made me want things that weren't possible between us. But I couldn't lie to him, or myself right now, either. "I feel the same way," I admitted, and swallowed hard. "But we both know we can't treat this like anything more than it is. An affair."

He stared at me for a long moment before he exhaled a deep breath. "You're right. I'm sorry. It's just...I've never felt a connection with a woman like this before."

I related to that one hundred percent, but instead of confirming anything emotional on my end—because yeah, those feelings for him were there and could spiral out of control if I let them—I opted to keep things focused on *him*. "I'm sure you've had a few solid relationships over the years."

He picked up my hand and just held it, the gesture so sweet it made my heart ache. "I had a girlfriend in high school for two years. It wasn't a mature connection as much as it was infatuation and young love. She broke up with me when I went into the Air Force." He shrugged his shoulder, clearly not affected by the end of that relationship. "And dating women while I was stationed all over the place in the military was difficult, though I did have a thing with another female officer for a while."

"A thing?" I asked curiously.

"A friendship with side benefits," he said as he absently stroked his fingers along my knuckles. "It was pretty mutual. We were together for a year and a half, then she met another guy, and that was the end of that."

He was so matter-of-fact about it all. "You weren't...hurt?"

"No, because I wasn't invested in the relationship. I mean, I cared for her, but I wasn't devastated when she moved on."

I realized that Jase had never been in a long-term, committed kind of relationship as an adult. I understood how being in the military could make it difficult to build a connection with a woman, but that knowledge made Jase seem even younger and the age difference between us seem even wider. Or maybe it just made me feel older than my thirty-five years, which wasn't a great feeling, either.

When I remained quiet, he went on. "This. Us. It just feels different in so many ways, and I wanted you to know that."

No, damn him. I didn't want to know that at all! Because that knowledge had the potential to mess with my head and my heart.

His gaze shifted to the clock on the wall, then back to me, and he smiled again. "Now I *really* have to go or I'm going to be late."

I could tell he was hesitant to leave after that huge reveal, but he leaned in and kissed me on the cheek, a sweet, chaste kiss that was so at odds with all the passion that had burned so hot and bright between us less than a half hour ago.

"I'll pick you up at seven for dinner tonight," he said as I walked with him to the door.

"Okay," I said before I could think better of my decision, because despite knowing how emotionally dangerous our relationship could become, I wasn't ready to walk away or let him go.

CHAPTER 12

Jase

"*I* have to say, for an older woman, she's fucking hot."

I had been just about ready to toss my metal ring across the yard to the fifty-point wooden peg in the grass thirty feet away when that crass comment abruptly stopped me.

I slowly straightened and glanced at Adam, a co-worker and the newest employee at Noble and Associates. The guy was thirty-two years old, had been in the Marines, and was trained in Intelligence Operations. On paper, he had all the qualifications of a competent and skilled operative, which was why Dean had hired him, but over the past month of getting to know Adam, I found there was just something about the guy that rubbed me the wrong way—like this immaturity that I'd seen glimpses of before.

And now, today, at a casual Saturday barbecue at Jillian and Dean's home that I had attended with Kendall, Adam was running his mouth and saying rude shit that I didn't appreciate one bit.

Wanting to give the other man the chance to rethink his stupid-ass remark, I tipped my head and spoke more calmly than I felt. "Excuse me?"

"Your girlfriend." Adam waved his fifth bottle of beer toward the back patio, where Kendall was sitting with the girls, drinking some kind of fruity concoction while laughing at something Raina said. "Isn't she, like, almost forty? At least, that's what I think one of the guys told me, though she doesn't look like it."

I clenched my jaw, my initial irritation

turning into full-blown anger. "Are you fucking kidding me right now, Adam?"

Eyes wide, the other man put his hands up in a gesture meant to calm me down. "Hey, it was a compliment. I mean, I hear older women are freaks between the sheets because they're at their sexual prime and want it all the time, so that makes you one lucky bastard."

My hands curled into fists, and it took supreme effort for me not to punch Adam in the face for being such an asshole. "Shut. The. Fuck. Up," I said succinctly, then dropped my metal ring on the grass and turned and walked away before I made a scene.

I exhaled a deep breath to ease the tension building in my chest and headed toward where the guys were standing around talking. Everyone had already eaten the barbecue ribs and sides that Dean and Jillian had served, and now it was just all about relaxing and enjoying the rest of the evening. Except I was far from feeling laid-back in any way whatsoever.

When Sawyer saw me approaching, he stepped away from the circle and met me a few feet away from everyone else, a concerned frown etching his features.

"Everything okay out there?" Sawyer asked as he glanced from me and back to Adam, who was now playing the ring toss game by himself. "Things were starting to look a little tense, and I get the feeling it had nothing to do with the lawn game you two were playing."

"I'll be fine," I said, trying to shake off my annoyance but failing. "Adam has no fucking filter, and I just need a couple of minutes to cool off after a few rude comments he made."

Sawyer raised a brow curiously. "About?"

"Kendall. And her age, along with some other insults." I jammed my fingers through my hair in agitation. "It was like we were back in high school and he was angling to get the dirty details of my relationship with her."

Sawyer shook his head. "Yeah, I've noticed that the guy is blunt, even juvenile at times despite *his* age, and it doesn't help that he's a drinker, which makes him even more obnoxious."

I glared back at Adam. "Having a few beers isn't an excuse to mouth off."

"I think it's worse than that," Sawyer said quietly. "A complaint came in on Friday from a client that Adam came to the job smelling like he'd had an alcoholic drink after his lunch break. Adam denied it, so Dean gave him a warning and put him on probation. The firm can't have that kind of liability."

"Well, he's definitely on his way to getting shit-faced here," I said, my tone disgusted.

We moved back to the group to join the conversation about a company's recent security breach that Mac had managed to avert. Eventually, Adam strolled up to the house, grabbed himself another beer, then joined the discussion. I deliberately kept a wide berth of the guy to avoid an altercation, though I was growing increasingly irked at the way Adam was watching Kendall from across the patio.

My gut churned, and that possessive feeling I harbored toward Kendall rose to the surface, the one that made me want to stake my claim on her right here and now. It was such a barbaric emotion, but over the past few weeks of dating her and sleeping with her and learning everything about her, that *need* for Kendall had only grown in depth. Not just my unquenchable desire for her but that elemental connection that was starting to make me feel anxious, like something profound was slipping through my fingers, even before it happened.

I didn't want to fucking lose her. That knowledge grew each day and night we spent together, morphing into an emotion that made me panic at times, because I knew I wasn't at a place in my life to give her all the things she wanted and deserved. Unfortunately, I couldn't change that fundamental gap between us that had *nothing* to do with our age difference, and neither could she.

She scooted away from the table she was sitting at, and while her girlfriends continued talking, she headed into the house by herself. That unsettling feeling in my stomach compelled me to follow her, to find a way to reassure myself that maybe, possibly, we could find a way to make a relationship between us work, even though I knew there was no easy solution, that we each had our own solid reasons for holding back.

At the moment, none of that mattered. Only Kendall did.

I expected her to go into the kitchen, but instead she veered down the hall to the bathroom. As I waited for her to exit, that unfamiliar restlessness inside me increased, and by the time she opened the door, I was desperate to slake the need billowing inside of me. And satisfy that soul-deep hunger that all started, and ended, with her.

She let out a gasp of surprise when she saw me standing there, and I crowded her right back into the bathroom, beyond caring that we were in my boss's house, and anyone could figure out what I was about to do to her. I couldn't wait, the urgency within me coiling so tight it threatened to break me.

"Jase, what are you doing?" she whispered as I shut and locked the door, then guided her back toward the vanity.

Grasping her waist, I lifted her so she was sitting on the smooth, flat surface, her legs dangling over the side, and ignored the *you can't be serious about having sex here* look on her face.

"I need you. Right here. Right now." As hard as my cock was, I realized that this moment, for me, wasn't all about sex and getting off. It was about knowing she was mine, and chasing away all those uncertainties lingering between us. Even if it was just for a few minutes.

I pushed her legs wide apart, grateful that she'd worn a lightweight dress, and stood between her spread thighs. Her lips parted to speak, and I plowed my hands into her hair, gripping the strands tight in my fist as I crushed my mouth to hers. Any protest she'd been about to make was lost in my all-consuming kiss, and instead she moaned and softened against me, and the hands she'd curled into my T-shirt released the material so she could slide her arms around my neck and return the embrace.

I dropped my eager hands to her thighs and quickly pushed the hem of her dress up around her hips, already knowing, and accepting, that this coupling was going to be fast and hot and hard—just how I needed it, *needed her*.

No thinking. Just feeling.

Tearing open the fly of my jeans, I shoved the denim and my briefs down over my ass until my cock sprang free. I managed to retrieve the one condom I had in my wallet, and even while she was kissing me, I managed to roll it down my erection. Reckless urgency drove me, and I slid my arms under her legs and lifted her knees, which tipped her body backwards. Her shoulders pressed against the mirror behind her, and my shaft was positioned between her thighs. The only thing separating us was her silky panties.

I met her gaze, the unconditional desire blazing in her eyes humbling me, arousing me, making me so delirious to be inside of her that my body shook. "Give me what I want, Kendall," I demanded in a low, rough voice. "Give me what I need."

She didn't hesitate to reach down and pull the front panel of her panties to the side, exposing her soft, gleaming pussy to me. Her other hand guided my cock forward, until the head was pressed a few inches inside her slick channel. With a brutal thrust of my hips, I was buried to the hilt, and I didn't stop there.

I continued pumping into her, hard and deep and fierce, and since her legs were draped over my forearms and spread wide apart, I was able to look down to where our bodies joined and watch as my cock drove in and out of her gorgeous cunt. She was so sweet and hot and lush and so damn addicting I didn't know if I'd ever get enough of her.

I could feel my orgasm building at the base

of my spine and refused to go over without her. "Touch yourself, Kendall," I ordered as I tunneled back into her tight, wet heat. "Make yourself come."

Her free hand moved down between her thighs, her fingers working her clit. A few balls-deep thrusts later and her body started to tremble. Her head fell back against the mirror, her face beautifully flushed with desire. Her lashes fluttered closed, and she bit her bottom lip to silence her passionate sounds, but a few escaped anyway in soft, panting moans as her inner muscles gripped and pulsed around my shaft.

Her rich, decadent scent filled my senses, and there was no holding back the blast of white-hot pleasure that surged through my balls and pulsed like liquid fury through my cock. "Fuck," I growled, as my hips jerked hard and fast against her and my release shot through me in an avalanche of sensation. "*Fuck*."

My entire body convulsed from the force of my orgasm. My head fell back, my back arching as I came so hard it felt as though it had been ripped from the very depths of my soul.

It took us both a few extra seconds to come back down from that adrenaline rush, to regulate our breathing so we weren't gulping for air. Bodies still joined, I leaned into her and touched my forehead to hers. The vision we each had for our futures might be years apart, but this was the one place where we were always in sync. The one thing that felt so perfectly right. This intimacy between us. The way she gave herself over to me so completely. And how calm and content I felt when I was with her.

In that moment, I knew I was falling in love with her, and there wasn't a damn thing I could do about it.

I lifted my head and stared into her soft green eyes, surprised by the concern I saw there. It startled me, how in tune to me she was. How in tune I was to her.

"Care to tell me what that was all about?" she asked softly.

She was smart enough to know that I hadn't locked her in the bathroom for a quick, hot fuck. Had obviously been aware of the tangle of emotions gnawing at me that I hadn't been able to contain. It was all so complicated. How could I explain what I didn't fully understand myself?

I looked away and shook my head. "No."

She didn't push me for an answer, and I was grateful. I moved away and took care of the condom while she put herself back together. Once we were both cleaned up and presentable, I grabbed her hand and laced our fingers together as I opened the door. Just outside the bathroom, Adam was leaning insolently against the opposite wall as if he'd been there a few minutes.

His eyes were glassy, and a smirk curled his lips as he leered at Kendall. "Damn, I need to find myself a cougar."

Kendall had teased me a few weeks earlier about being a cougar, but knowing that Adam meant it in a purely nasty, derogatory way made my temper spike. I didn't flip my shit easily, but I was so done with Adam and his mouth. Releasing Kendall's hand, I took the three steps to Adam, curled my fists into his T-shirt, and slammed him up against the wall.

I heard Kendall call my name from behind

me in a panicked voice, but my blood was at a boil and nothing mattered but putting this asshole in his place. "You need to shut your fucking mouth, Adam."

"Maybe she'd like to shut it for me," he sneered, his words a slur as he pushed at my chest, which didn't so much as budge me. "When she's done with you, I can show her what it's like to fuck someone more her own age."

Kendall's soft gasp of shock put me over the edge, and I slammed my fist into Adam's jaw. The other man's face snapped to the side and he grunted, but in the next instant, he exploded and barreled his entire body into me, knocking us both to the floor. Punches were thrown, knuckles connected with flesh, along with body shots to the ribs. Even intoxicated, Adam was a well-trained and formidable opponent.

I ignored Kendall's shouts for us to stop, and just as I was about to land a solid punch to Adam's gut, I was yanked off of the other man by the back of my shirt, with a strength and force that brought me all the way up to my feet. Adam remained flat on his back on the floor, glaring up at me belligerently, but at least

Adam had a bloody nose and his jaw would no doubt throb like a son-of-a-bitch, I thought with satisfaction.

Sawyer had been the one to drag me off of Adam, and Logan gave the other man a hand to help him up. Adam swayed on his feet before gaining his balance, then set his shoulders back in a cocky stance, and I was sorely tempted to knock Adam back on his ass again.

"What the fuck is going on?" Dean barked in that authoritative tone of his. His hands were jammed on his hips, and his expression was pissed as he looked from me to Adam and back again.

Dean waited for an answer, but I knew my boss wasn't a patient man when it came to petty shit like this. "Nothing's going on," I said, realizing that the fight, or Kendall's frantic screaming, had pretty much drawn everyone into the house to see what was causing such a ruckus. The girls were circled around Kendall trying to console her, while the men were keeping a close eye on me and Adam to make sure that nobody tried to throw a last punch.

"Nothing?" Dean repeated incredulously.

"Are you two beating the shit out of each other for fun, then?"

Adam dragged the back of his hand across his face to wipe away the blood coming out of his nose. He didn't utter a word. Instead, his gaze mocked me as if to dare me to reveal what had prompted the brawl.

He called Kendall a cougar... Yeah, that sounded stupid and petty and juvenile. But that comment on top of all the other insults Adam had spewed out in the yard, and I had blown a very short fuse. Even Kendall, who was looking at me from across the room with wide, bewildered eyes, clearly didn't understand my outburst, either.

When neither man offered up an explanation, Dean exhaled a harsh breath. "You both need to go home and cool off. We'll talk about this at the office Monday morning."

I knew a dismissal when I heard one. Dean was a fair man, but he didn't tolerate his men butting heads and fist fighting. Especially in his home.

Adam nodded and started for the door, and I couldn't resist saying, "After six beers, don't you think you should call a cab or have someone drive you home?"

Dean's gaze swung back around to Adam to assess the other man's inebriated state. He must have seen something that alerted him, because Dean swore beneath his breath before he addressed Adam. "You're not driving yourself home."

If looks could kill, Adam's death glare would have murdered me on the spot. But as much as Adam believed my remark had been a petty one, the thought of Adam driving under the influence and possibly causing an accident didn't sit well with me at all.

Mac stepped forward. "I'll drop Adam off on my way home. He can come and get his car tomorrow."

The party broke up, with everyone deciding it was time to head home, too. I apologized to both Jillian and Dean for my behavior, because I knew I'd been out of line. The drive back to my place with Kendall was quiet, and not in a good way. I was silent because I didn't want to talk about what had happened with Adam, and she was, undoubtedly, mulling over what had really caused me to come unhinged on my co-worker.

I parked my truck in the garage, and we both went through the door that led directly into the kitchen. We'd been staying at my place over the past week. I'd just recently purchased the house in a middle-class neighborhood, and it was much bigger and roomier than Kendall's apartment. Things between us had become routine and comfortable, but I had a feeling I'd just shaken the status quo.

She set her purse on the counter, then followed me into the master bedroom, then the adjoining bathroom. I'd intended to take a shower, but she obviously had a different agenda.

"Let me take a look at that cut by your right eye," she said evenly, in a way that made it difficult for me to read her mood.

I frowned. I hadn't even realized I had any open wounds—bruises by tomorrow, absolutely—and I absently touched my finger to where she'd indicated. The spot right at my brow was tender and sore, like a raw scrape, and I winced. Sure enough, Adam had somehow managed to break open my skin with his fist during our scuffle.

"I'm fine," I said with a shake of my head. "It's just a small cut."

Her lips pursed and her eyes flashed tenaciously. "Sit down and let me clean it up so it doesn't get infected."

Ms. Bossy pointed to the toilet seat, and with a sigh, I sat down on the closed lid as she took charge. I watched her retrieve a bottle of hydrogen peroxide from the medicine cabinet and a bag of cotton balls from the drawer. She washed her hands, then moved to my right side to examine the cut a bit closer.

"What happened back at Jillian's with Adam?" she finally asked as she doused a cotton ball with the antiseptic.

She asked the question in such a calm manner, and I wasn't sure what to make of her reserved demeanor, which made me feel distinctly uneasy. "The guy is a certified prick and has a problem running off at the mouth."

She applied the wet cotton to my open cut, and I flinched and hissed out a sharp breath at the initial sting. "Shit, that hurts," I muttered.

"It's a little deeper than you think," she said,

ignoring my grimace of pain as she dabbed and wiped at the wound again. "But at least it's not deep enough to require stitches."

Things between us grew quiet as she continued tending to the abrasion. I didn't care for the tension between the two of us but wasn't sure what to do or say to alleviate it.

After a long stretch of silence, she finally spoke again. "When we came out of the bathroom and Adam made the cougar comment, I got the impression that wasn't the first time he'd provoked you about our relationship."

As much as I wanted to spare her the details, I wasn't going to lie to her. "No, it wasn't."

Finished cleaning my cut, she dabbed a bit of Neosporin ointment on the scrape, then started putting everything away. "What other things did he say?"

Shit. I so didn't want to go there with her, didn't want her to have to hear those ignorant comments. "Kendall..."

She turned around to face me and crossed her arms over her chest. "Tell me, Jase. If it was bad enough for you to have to jump to my defense the way you did, I have a right to know why."

I pinched the bridge of my nose with my fingers and closed my eyes for a moment. All those uncertain feelings from earlier came rushing to the forefront again, along with a dose of fear...the fear of losing her once we had this conversation. I knew the possibility existed, knew I was about to touch on all the issues that would cause her to withdraw and build those walls between us again.

I opened my eyes and lifted my head, already seeing the cautious look in her eyes. "Let's just say Adam made some very crude remarks about you being an older woman, and I'm not going to repeat his comments word for word, so don't ask."

"I *am* older than you. By *eight* years," she said, her voice tight, as if she was trying to hold back her own swell of emotion. "What are we doing, Jase?" She shook her head in frustration. "You *should* be with someone younger and more your age, and I need to—"

"*Don't* say it," I snapped, my tone harsher than I intended. She gave me a painfully heartbreaking look before turning around and walking out of the bathroom.

I jammed my hands through my hair in aggravation. I hadn't meant to snap, but I wasn't ready to hear those inevitable words that would have Kendall walking out of my life. Not yet. Maybe not ever.

It was such a selfish thought considering I couldn't make her any promises.

CHAPTER 13

Kendall

With the day almost done at Pure Bliss, I sat in my studio office, working to finish editing the pictures from a recent boudoir photo shoot before I left for the evening. I was meeting Jase at his place in an hour for dinner, so I still had about forty minutes before I closed shop and headed out.

Four days had passed since the incident at Dean and Jillian's, and since that night, there'd been a definite change between us. It was as though that evening, and our conversation back at his place, had initiated the beginning of the end. Things had gone from comfortable to strained, and we both knew why. It had nothing to do with Jase's altercation with Adam—that had just been the catalyst—and everything to do with the fact that we were at different points in our lives. We were standing at a fork in the road with two contrasting paths leading in opposite directions.

We were also at a stalemate because neither one of us could bring ourselves to make the next logical move. We hadn't spoken about the huge elephant in the room, had avoided any discussion about the future, but I felt the shift between us in the tentative way we glanced at one another and in the quiet tension between us. Even the sex had changed. Having Jase inside me had become more about the slow, intimate pleasure of making love rather than indulging in the raw, primal, erotic edge he'd introduced me to. The passion between us hadn't abated; it had just transformed into something deeper and more emotional.

It was as though we were slowly saying good-bye, and that knowledge caused a lump to form in my throat and my heart to tighten in my chest. We were both aware that the gradual process of letting go had started, and even though I'd only been with Jase a few weeks, I already knew this separation was going to be even more painful than my divorce had been. If we'd met at a different point in our lives, or our futures had been more aligned, I was pretty sure that Jase would have been *the one*. But I didn't have years to wait to start the family I wanted so badly, and he wasn't ready to make that kind of commitment. I had eight years on Jase, and at the moment, I felt the weight, and distance, of every one of them.

I should have known that I wasn't the type of woman who could have an affair, give my body to a man, and not get emotionally attached. Especially when that man was a perfect match for me in so many ways—except the most essential. Falling in love with Jase had already happened, and those growing feelings scared the crap out of me, since we both knew there was no way our relationship would work for the long haul.

The sound of the door opening into the studio brought me back to the present. I saved the photo I'd been working on, put the file away so nothing got accidentally deleted, and headed out to the reception area. A woman stood there. She was meticulously, elegantly dressed. Her purse was a designer label, and I was fairly certain that the glossy pumps on her feet had cost a small fortune. As well as the huge diamond sparkling on her ring finger.

The woman looked well-kept and wealthy, but her expression was tentative and nervous as she watched me approach. I didn't think she was there for the receptionist position I still needed to fill, so I assumed she was a potential client and quickly tried to put her at ease.

"Hi, I'm Kendall, the owner of Pure Bliss Boudoir Photography." I extended my hand in greeting, which the other woman hesitantly shook, her fingers soft and cool to the touch. "And you are?"

"Lauren," she replied reluctantly.

"Nice to meet you, Lauren," I went on, my tone warm and welcoming. "Are you interested in a boudoir session?"

Her brown eyes grew round as she hastily shook her head. "I…uh…no."

I tipped my head and smiled. "I also do

regular photography and portraits if that's something you need."

Another rapid shake of her head as the woman clung to the purse hanging from her shoulder. "No, I actually need to ask you a question. I'm hoping you can help me with something."

Lauren seemed so distraught that I felt compelled to do anything I could to alleviate her anxiety. "Sure. What can I do for you?"

The woman reached into her purse and withdrew a small, wallet-sized photo. One that I recognized immediately. It was a sexy, erotic shot of the "headless" couple—Stacie and Richard.

My stomach pitched queasily. Dreading where I suspected this conversation was about to go, I swallowed hard and raised my gaze back to the other woman's. Her eyes were filled with the kind of pain that I knew and understood all too well. The pain of betrayal.

"I need to know if the man in this picture is my husband." Lauren's hand shook as she held up the incriminating shot. "The photo has your studio name on the back, which is how I knew the picture was taken here. Is his name Richard?"

As much as this woman needed me to verify who the man was, I couldn't. It was a part of the contract I signed with my clients to ensure their privacy. To divulge that information, for any reason, could damage my reputation, and it was a personal risk I couldn't take because of my business.

Yet my heart hurt for the woman standing in front of me. For what she had to be feeling at the moment, because I had been there myself. "I'm very sorry," I said, not confirming or denying what the woman needed to know. "I can't share client information."

Just the fact that I hadn't jumped to assure the woman that the man's name *wasn't* Richard —which wouldn't have violated the contract terms—was enough to tell Lauren all she needed to know.

I really looked at the woman for the first time. She was probably in her mid-forties... unlike Stacie, who was young and in her twenties. I recalled my last conversation with Stacie, how the woman had made the comment that nothing was guaranteed until she had a ring on her finger, and how she was waiting for Richard to get his shit together…obviously as in divorce his wife. Which it seemed Richard hadn't been in any hurry to do. But now I understood why they'd wanted no faces in the shots, not that it mattered in the end if Richard had left it somewhere for his wife to discover.

"Where did you find the photo?" I asked softly, giving the woman the opportunity to talk if she wanted to.

"In his wallet, the idiot," Lauren replied, some of her anger coming through. "I had a feeling he was seeing someone else, but he always had a ready excuse for his behavior. Then, when I found this photo, even though you can't see his face, I didn't bother asking him questions, because I know he'd deny everything and try to make me feel like I'm being overly dramatic, just like he's done with everything else in our twenty-year marriage."

As Lauren spoke, her initial hurt and uncertainty shifted into disgust and resentment. Her shoulders straightened, and her chin lifted. "But you know what? I'm through being placated by that bastard, and we have a prenup that will string him up by the balls. I just needed some kind of evidence that he's screwing around on me, and now that he is, I'll make sure a private investigator gets all the incriminating information I need before I contact a divorce attorney."

By the time Lauren left the studio, now with purpose and determination, I felt drained. My earlier thoughts and issues in regard to my relationship with Jase now seemed even more glaring. I'd honestly believed I'd gotten beyond my insecurities about my ex-husband's betrayal, about not being young enough or good enough for Drew. But hearing Lauren's story only brought up those uncertainties all over again.

I didn't believe that Jase would ever cheat on me, but it was just one more thing that kept me guarded and unable to commit. Not that committing was even an option when the man I was in love with wasn't ready for marriage. Or children.

CHAPTER 14

Jase

I stared absently into my refrigerator, trying to figure out what to make myself and Kendall for dinner. I wasn't in the mood to cook. Hell, I wasn't even in the mood to eat considering how shitty my afternoon had been. I was seriously thinking about ordering takeout when I heard Kendall come through the front door. A few seconds later, she walked into the kitchen, and I took one look at her somber expression and my stomach twisted into a huge knot of apprehension.

She put her purse down on the counter, her walls a mile high. But that didn't stop me from walking over to her and pulling her into my embrace. Her body was stiff at first, but she eventually laid her head on my chest, wrapped her arms around my waist, and hugged me back.

It should have been a comforting embrace, but it felt as though she was trying desperately to cling to something elusive and fleeting. I knew exactly what that intangible thing was. I just didn't want to face it, and apparently, neither did she.

After a while I pulled back and she glanced up at me. She must have seen the irritation still lingering from that afternoon's conversation with Dean and Mac at the office, because she frowned in concern.

"Looks like you had a crappy day, too. Everything okay?" she asked as she tried to casually slip out of my arms.

I let her go and leaned my backside against the counter. I hated when she moved away from me, because the distance suddenly seemed more than just physical. But that's the way it had been between us lately, and every day it only seemed to get worse. I knew it was her way of protecting her emotions, a way of keeping her heart safe. I couldn't blame her for that, because I was trying to do the same.

I exhaled a deep breath and answered her question. "Adam and I *finally* got summoned to Dean's office." It was three days later than expected, because everyone had had different agendas and Dean and Mac had been out of the office until this afternoon.

"And?" she asked, her eyes wide with worry. "You didn't get fired, did you?"

I knew that was her biggest concern, that my impulsive actions on Saturday—on her behalf—would cost me my job. "No. But Adam did."

I saw the questions in her eyes and continued on. "We both got a lecture and a warning since the altercation happened outside of work. But then Mac asked Adam to take a Breathalyzer test, right then and there, and he completely flipped out and refused. I smelled some kind of alcohol on Adam, too, when he walked into the office, so he'd obviously been drinking again. On the job."

Kendall folded her arms across her chest and winced. "Wow."

I casually slid my hands into the front pockets of my jeans. "I think Dean and Mac realized the drinking was a much bigger problem for Adam, and might be Adam's way of dealing with PTSD, which is common. Dean offered him treatment, but Adam refused. So, they terminated him, and he came unglued and went into a rage, verbally *and* physically."

Shock etched her expression, even as she scanned my features with worry. "Did you and Adam get into another fight?"

"No. Mac restrained him pretty quickly, and I left the office so they could deal with him. But overall, the whole situation was pretty bad."

"Not a good day for either one of us, I guess," she said quietly.

She didn't say anything more, but I knew whatever was on her mind was weighing heavily on her. "What happened?"

She rubbed her fingers across her forehead, but that did nothing to erase the troubled lines of distress I saw there. "Right before I was ready to leave the studio this evening, a woman came in and showed me a boudoir picture I'd taken, of her husband and the younger woman he was having an affair with."

Oh, shit. I knew exactly where this was heading, that today's incident had caused her past to clash with the present, with me caught somewhere in the middle. "And?"

She met my gaze in silence. But I was going to make her *say* it. "And it just made me think long and hard about you and me and our affair."

Despite the dread twisting through me, I still tried to avoid the inevitable. "The difference is, *you're* not married."

"No, but I want to be," she said softly, meaningfully. "Very much. I want a husband and a family, and I don't want to wait, I *can't* wait, another five years for that to happen. You *know* that."

Yes, she'd been honest with me from the beginning, but that didn't stop me from feeling as though I'd taken a blow to the stomach. Panic and denial clashed inside of me, and I instinctively started toward her. "Kendall—"

She held up a hand to stop my words and my approach. "No, Jase. We can't keep doing this." The pain in her eyes spoke volumes and slayed me in a way nothing else ever had. "The feelings I have for you...it's all getting so complicated, and I just can't do this anymore."

The fear of losing her forever had me in a stranglehold, and desperation took hold. "You can walk away so easily?"

"Nothing about this is easy. For either one of us," she acknowledged, acute sadness filling her eyes. "But you aren't ready to settle down, and if I stay in this relationship, I know I'll come to resent the situation, possibly even you, and that's not how I want to remember you...or us."

I couldn't even argue with her, because she was right. About everything. She knew what she wanted for her future and was at the point in her life to make all those things happen. I wasn't. And wouldn't be for years. For all of my adult life, I'd had a plan, and I'd yet to stray from that path. My own unstable and painful childhood had dictated everything I'd ever done since the age of eighteen. The military had been a starting place, the first step in building a future for myself, and at some point, that would include a wife and family. But I was just now starting a new career, had just purchased a new house, and marriage and kids were still a ways down the road for me—and longer than Kendall should have to wait.

That damned age difference I hadn't thought mattered just kept coming back to haunt me. First with Adam's asshole comments and then with this cheating husband...who no doubt reminded Kendall of her own past. I knew we'd been on borrowed time, but I'd thought I could string things out longer, have more time with her...

Fuck.

The defeat I felt in that moment was crushing.

The resignation in her gaze was equally excruciating.

"I should go," she said, her voice as ragged and vulnerable as my emotions.

Before she could react, I closed the distance between us, plowed my fingers through her hair, and brought her mouth to mine for a hot, deep, soul-baring kiss. She didn't resist me. Her lips parted, accepting the sweep of my tongue, while I took full possession of her mouth with a fierce groan. I tasted her one last time, memorizing the flavor of her, the scent of her, and knew it would never, ever be enough.

I couldn't have her, but there would be no forgetting her, either.

CHAPTER 15

Kendall

I stared at the plastic stick in my hand in shock, not sure whether I should laugh or cry at the news I'd just been delivered. Or maybe do both at the same time. That's how conflicted I felt about the entire situation.

I was two weeks past due on my period. While I blamed overall stress for the delay, I was never late, and it had taken me this long to gather up the courage to confirm what I already knew in my heart and face the changes already happening with my body. The nausea in the mornings had been my first clue, followed by my tender and swollen breasts that were incredibly sensitive to the touch. And despite a solid eight hours of sleep a night, I felt exhausted all day long.

"Well, what does it say?" Stephanie asked anxiously from where she was pacing in my small living room. My good friend was there to offer moral support, and she chewed on her thumbnail as she waited for me to answer.

"It's positive," I whispered, still trying to work through the array of emotions filtering through me. Joy. Fear. And regret that this hadn't happened differently. The latter thought made my throat tight with heartache. "I'm pregnant."

"Oh, wow." Stephanie came up to me, her gaze filled with a combination of awe and concern. "You're going to have a baby."

I glanced back at the pregnancy test, but the results remained the same. "So it seems."

It had been three weeks since Jase and I had broken up, and I hadn't seen or talked to him since. I'd asked for a clean break, and he'd respected my request, even though it had been one of the most difficult decisions I'd ever made. But I knew it would be impossible to have Jase in my life in any capacity and not grow more attached or, worse, fall deeper in love with the man. The fact that I'd let my emotions get so tangled up in what should have been an uncomplicated affair proved that much.

Stephanie sat down on the couch. "Do you know when it might have happened?"

"No." Placing the incriminating test strip on the coffee table, I settled onto the cushion next to my friend, still feeling dazed. "I went off the pill when I divorced Drew, but Jase used protection every single time, so getting pregnant was something I didn't think was even feasible." Until this morning, when I'd Googled the possibility of getting pregnant while using a condom and learned that, yes, it did happen, with breakage and deterioration being the most common issues. It was a small percentage, but it did occur. Even Jase himself had been a product of failed birth control, which made my current predicament even more ironic.

Stephanie's gaze turned sympathetic as she placed her hand over mine. "Just goes to show you, no form of birth control is one hundred percent effective."

"Except abstinence," I said with a wry twist of my lips.

Stephanie laughed and shook her head. "Nah, there's no fun in that." Then she grew serious once more, her eyes softening with wonder. "I can't believe you're going to have a baby."

The stunning realization was slowly sinking in, and I knew once this initial shock wore off, I'd accept this child for the blessing it was and be delighted by the prospect of being a mom. But the irony of the situation wasn't lost on me, either.

For so many years, all I'd wanted was a baby. My wish had finally come true, except for the fact that the father of my child wasn't ready to start a family, and I'd never use an accidental pregnancy to force him into a marriage he didn't want and wasn't ready for.

"What are you going to do about Jase?" Stephanie asked, as if reading my mind.

I didn't think twice about my answer. "I'm going to tell him about the baby because as the father he has the right to know and be a part of the child's life in whatever way he decides. But I'm fully prepared to be a single mom in every way." And I'd make sure Jase also knew that just because I was pregnant didn't mean I had any expectations of him being a part of my life during the next nine months. He didn't need to be there for the doctor's appointments or feel obligated to check on me. In fact, the less contact we had, the better for my heart and emotional state. I didn't want him around knowing it was only out of obligation, and I didn't want the painful reminder about what could have been if we'd both wanted the same things.

"You know all of us girls are here for you and the baby, no matter what you need," Stephanie said, giving my hand a comforting squeeze. "You won't be alone for any part of this."

"I know." A swell of tears filled my eyes. I was so grateful to have such amazing women as friends, but I was also incredibly sad that I wouldn't be able to share this experience, in its entirety, with Jase. The one person who mattered the most.

I pressed a hand to my still-flat stomach

and smiled for the first time that day, awed that a little life was growing inside of me. Raising a child alone wouldn't be easy, and it certainly wasn't what I'd envisioned for myself, but I had absolutely no regrets about the baby I was now carrying.

CHAPTER 16

Jase

I sat at the small table at the coffee house where Kendall had asked to meet me after work—via a short, impersonal text. After three long weeks of not seeing her or hearing her voice, I was anxious to watch her walk into the cafe. I had no idea what she wanted, but a part of me hoped that she was just as miserable without me as I was without her. That maybe she wanted to try and make a relationship work, just as badly as I did.

Our time apart had been excruciating,

and every single night, I'd had to battle the urge to pick up the phone and call her. To respect the decision she'd made to end things between us. But as each day passed without her in it, I couldn't help but wonder if letting her go was the single stupidest mistake I'd made in my entire life. That my unwillingness to compromise might have cost me the best thing that had ever happened to me. It was a painful thought I struggled with every night, with no easy answer or life-altering revelation by morning.

My days were long. My nights were empty. I'd never had an issue being alone or by myself —my whole childhood I'd been a solitary kind of kid, then man—yet my big house seemed quieter. More desolate. It was missing warmth and laughter and *life*. There was no joy or excitement in the things I'd accomplished, and no strong motivation for all the things I still wanted to pursue before settling down with a wife and family.

Because the one and only woman I'd ever wanted all of that with had quite possibly already slipped through my fingers. Or maybe not, I prayed as I continued to wait for Kendall to arrive.

Beneath the table, my leg twitched nervously. My stomach felt like I was on a roller coaster of highs and lows, and seeing Kendall, and being able to gauge her mood and her reason for meeting me, would be the deciding factor of whether the ride would soar with relief or plummet to the ground.

She finally pushed through the main door and walked inside. She stopped to glance around to find me, giving me a few precious seconds to take in how beautiful she looked in a pale pink blousy top and a pair of white capri pants. When her gaze turned in my direction, I lifted my hand to get her attention.

I watched her take a deep breath before heading my way, and as she neared, I couldn't help but think how fragile and vulnerable she looked. And very tired. There was no easy, welcoming smile on her lips. Her eyes lacked their usual vibrancy, and her complexion looked paler than normal. There was no indi-cation that she was happy or excited to see me. No, if anything, her expression reflected a sense of dread.

I felt the thrill ride I'd been on start to crash and burn. Yes, she looked as miserable as I felt, but it was the apprehension in the way she approached my table that indicated she wasn't here to confess how much she missed me.

She slid into the chair across from me and gave me a forced smile. "Hi, Jase."

"Hi," I replied, and because there was no missing the awkward tension between us, I sought to put her at ease. "Can I get you something to eat or drink?"

"No, thanks." Her voice was too damned polite, and she looked everywhere but at me. "This won't take long."

I couldn't begin to imagine what she'd come there to tell me, but the fact that she looked so distraught and couldn't even look me in the eyes caused me concern. Instinct had me reaching across the table and settling my hand on top of hers. "Kendall…is everything okay?"

"I…" She visibly swallowed and finally met my gaze, unable to hide the anguish shimmering in the depths. "I'm pregnant."

I blinked at her, shock rendering me mute. It was the last thing I'd expected to hear, and it took my brain a few extra seconds to process her words. "You're pregnant?" I echoed dumbly as I gradually pulled my hand away from hers. "How..." My voice trailed off, severing the stupid question of *how did that happen?* Instead, I said in a low tone to keep the conversation private, "We used protection every single time."

"Yes, we did," she said, as if understanding my confusion. "But as you well know, accidents happen."

Fuck. I knew all about accidents, because I *was* one. Actually, according to my parents, I'd been a *mistake*, and that memory felt like a punch to the gut.

"I took a home pregnancy test first a few days ago, then went to my doctor yesterday to confirm the pregnancy before I said anything to you," she said, wringing her hands nervously together. "I'm about five weeks along."

I slumped back in my chair and stared at her, not knowing what to say. So many thoughts and feelings were flying through my head. Stunned disbelief. A spark of panic. And overwhelming fear, because I wasn't ready for *a baby*, mentally or emotionally. The realization that I was going to have a kid was terrifying and clashed with everything I'd mapped out so strategically in my mind.

"I know this isn't something either of us planned on, but you have a right to know about the baby," she rushed on, her words spilling out of her quickly and leaving me no room to reply or ask questions. "I know you aren't prepared for this… You said you aren't ready for a family at this point in your life, so I want you to know…I don't expect anything from you. I plan on raising the child on my own. But if you want to be part of the baby's life, we can contact a lawyer to work out visitation rights and custody issues, and anything else that needs to be addressed. I just wanted to make sure you knew I was pregnant so you can make your own decisions about what part you want to play in the child's life." She finished in a rush, the entire explanation clearly planned out ahead of time.

I couldn't keep up with everything she was saying. I hadn't had time to digest the information like she had, and my head was spinning as I tried to come up with some kind of response. But all I could focus on was her announcement that she planned on raising the child on her own and didn't need anything from me.

She abruptly grabbed her purse and stood up, nearly knocking down her chair in the process. "I need to go."

"Wait." I jumped to my feet just as quickly, my heart hammering in my chest because I wasn't ready for her to go. I stepped toward her. "Kendall—" We needed to talk...but where did I start when I still hadn't fully accepted or even processed that she was *pregnant*.

"Don't." Eyes wide and swimming with tears, she took a meaningful step back. "I can't handle anything more right now," she said, her voice tight.

She turned around and hurried out of the café without giving me a chance to think, let alone have my say.

I hadn't seen Kendall in three weeks, missed her like crazy, and had hoped she'd come here to tell me she wanted to give us a chance. Instead she'd informed me she was pregnant, announced she didn't need or want anything from me, and disappeared as quickly as she'd come, leaving me feeling as though I'd been ripped through a tornado of emotions and left devastated in the aftermath.

* * *

"Want to talk about it?"

I glanced at Sawyer, who'd asked me to join him for a beer after work. Considering I had nothing to go home to, I had agreed, though there hadn't been much conversation between the two of us up to this point. I knew I'd been moody, testy even, since meeting with Kendall three nights ago. I had no idea why Sawyer would want to subject himself to my crappy attitude, and now the other man was asking if I wanted to spill my guts.

"Talk about what?" I asked, deliberately vague. I wasn't ready to divulge my impending fatherhood to anyone just yet. Not until I figured out what I was going to do about Kendall, and the baby.

Sawyer pinned me with a direct, *don't bother to bullshit me* kind of look. "The fact that you're going to be a daddy."

My brows snapped together in a frown. "How the fuck did you know?"

My friend took a long sip of his beer and shrugged. "You have to remember that my fiancée is part of that close-knit posse of girl-friends that includes Kendall, and those women are fiercely protective of each other," he said, reminding me that Sawyer had personal experience with the group. "And since I'm the one Paige comes home to at night, anything she wants to rant about filters down to me. Sorry to break it to you, but *you* were the latest rant."

What the fuck? "I was?" I asked, bristling.

The corner of Sawyer's mouth quirked up in a humorous grin. "I think the exact comment she made to me was, 'Jase needs to step up and be a man.'"

I opened my mouth with a nasty retort to that, but Sawyer held up his hand and cut me off before continuing. "I'm not here to judge, because that was a serious bombshell Kendall dropped on you, and you need to do what's best for you. But I just thought you might need a listening ear."

I appreciated Sawyer's friendship, but I couldn't let Paige's comment slide. "You can let your girlfriend know that I plan to man up. I'm not going to turn my back on my own kid." The thought had never crossed my mind. I just hadn't known how to approach Kendall or what to say, not to mention she hadn't been ready to really talk to me, either. So I'd taken the time to wrap my head around things and settle on a plan.

"So you're going to be a part-time father, then?"

Fuck no. That was too cold and uncaring, too close to what I'd experienced as a child. My parents had been married, but for the most part, I had been an afterthought, and I never wanted a kid of mine to ever feel that they were an inconvenience. That's exactly what it would be like with a shared custody agreement, and that thought made me feel sick to my stomach.

"Kendall made it very clear that she's going to raise the baby on her own, and that she doesn't need anything from me." I braced both elbows on the bar top and ran all ten fingers though my hair in frustration. "I was so fucking shocked by the announcement I couldn't think straight, let alone come up with a reply...and then she was gone. She had *days* to come to terms with the fact that she was pregnant, and I had five goddamn minutes."

"Yeah, not cool, man," Sawyer agreed. "But I'm sure it wasn't easy for her to tell you, either."

"I know." I'd seen the pained look in Kendall's eyes, having to tell me something I'd already made clear I didn't want at this point in my life. I released a heavy sigh. "This pregnancy wasn't something I was expecting at all. Hell, we broke up because she wanted to start a family, and I wasn't ready to give her that kind of commitment."

Sawyer waited for me to look at him before he asked, "And now that you have a kid on the way?"

"I'm scared as shit about being a father right now."

Sawyer smirked. "It's not like you can stop the kid from coming."

"You know what I mean," I said, glaring at him for his sarcasm. "It's complicated. Kendall had issues about us that went beyond bad timing. Kendall was married for ten years, and her husband led her to believe that they'd start a family once he was out of med school, finished with his internships, and all their debt was paid off. For ten years she supported him and worked two jobs to pay off their outrageous school loans, and six months later, he leaves her for a younger woman who is pregnant with his baby."

"What an asshole," Sawyer said.

"Yeah. The thing is, she thinks our age difference is an issue. That one day I'll realize I want someone closer to my own age."

"That's just fucking ridiculous. Although now I get why you went after Adam the way you did."

I nodded. "Yeah. He hit a sore spot. Kendall is thirty-five and at the point in her life where she wants to be married and start a family. And after what her ex put her through, she deserves that. But I'm twenty-seven, just out of the military, and I'm starting to build a career, which in turn will enable me to support a family...someday."

"Hate to break it to you, buddy. That someday is now."

"Would you cut it with the sarcasm already?" I muttered. "I've always envisioned being firmly established in every aspect of my life before doing any of those things, and I'm not there yet. So we broke up."

Sawyer frowned at me. "Jesus, you can't always *plan* everything. Life is going to throw you unexpected curves, and sometimes you just have to go with the flow and not because it's all part of some step-by-step outline you've been following for years."

"Yeah, I got that now," I said to my friend. "I pretty much came to the same conclusion while tossing and turning in bed the pasts few nights."

The two of us were quiet for a few minutes, then Sawyer asked, "Do you love her?"

"Yes," I said without hesitation. I already knew that I'd fucked up. Badly. And I was afraid that I was too late in telling Kendall how I truly felt about her. She'd think I was stepping up because of the baby...and I couldn't deny that had been the impetus for me to think with my heart and not my head.

But I knew now I couldn't live without her. Baby or no baby, I wanted her in my life. Even if she weren't pregnant, I'd come to realize I'd give her the family she wanted sooner than I planned because a future without her would devastate me. I wanted the same things she did, with her. And only with her. To hell with my damned timeline and plans.

"You know, I almost lost Paige after what her sister did to the two of us," Sawyer said quietly. "And for that year and a half that we spent apart, I had so many regrets. But I was lucky that things worked out for us, that I had a second chance to tell her all the things I hadn't said before I left for the military. Whatever you do, make sure you don't look back and regret the choice you made. Make the right choice, right now."

"My choice is Kendall, and the baby," I said, and knew it was true from the moment she'd said she was pregnant with my baby. I shouldn't have let her walk out on me at the cafe, but dammit, I was entitled to thinking time, too. I glanced at Sawyer. "I'm just not sure *her* choice is me."

"If you want her badly enough, then fight for her," Sawyer said, speaking from experience.

"Oh, I plan to." Somehow I'd convince Kendall that it was our time apart that had shown me the error of my thinking, that I loved her for her, that the baby was an early bonus, not the obligation that had brought me back into her life.

For the first time in three days, I felt like I had a purpose...that I wasn't deviating from the plan I'd had for my life but was creating a new blueprint for happiness, one that made more sense. And would make me happier than I'd ever imagined being. Now I just had to convince Kendall to give me the chance to prove what she, and this baby, meant to me.

CHAPTER 17

Kendall

The brisk knock on my door startled me. I'd just sat down with a bowl of chicken noodle soup and crackers, and I wasn't expecting anyone. I'd come home from work later than normal and exhausted, and I knew I was probably going to have to hire another photographer, on top of a front-end girl, to help me get through the next few months.

I'd taken a warm shower, changed into a pair of old, comfy sweats, and washed off my makeup and put my hair up in a ponytail. After dinner, I'd planned on heading to bed and maybe read for a bit until I couldn't keep my eyes open any longer—which usually happened pretty quickly these days.

Another quick knock and I scooted away from my small kitchen table and headed to the door. I looked through the peephole, and my heart picked up its beat when I saw Jase standing on the other side of the threshold.

I closed my eyes, pressed my head against the door, and exhaled a deep breath. After the way I'd run out on Jase at the cafe, I'd been expecting this confrontation. I just wasn't sure I was prepared to deal with the emotional aspect of our conversation, the very painful discussion of how this baby would probably be raised by two separate people in a shared custody agreement, instead of being raised in the kind of stable, loving, two-parent home I'd always hoped for and dreamed of.

I opened the door, wishing I didn't look so frumpy when he looked so damned gorgeous. A pang of longing struck me as I stared into his warm brown eyes. I'd missed him so much over these past weeks. God, was I really going to be able to get through the next seven months and beyond without him in my life on a daily basis?

The thought of what I'd be dealing with all by myself suddenly seemed so overwhelming and daunting, but then again, I'd faced other devastating adversities and had survived. I'd get through this, too, and have a beautiful baby at the end to make it all worthwhile.

"Can I come in?" Jase asked since my mind had gone off on a tangent and I hadn't said a word to him yet.

"Yes, of course." My tone was polite as I moved aside to let him enter.

"I'm sorry I didn't call first." He stepped into the adjoining kitchen, then turned around to face me. "I was afraid that if I gave you too much time to think, you wouldn't let me in the door." The half smile he gave me helped to ease my nerves.

"You're always welcome here," I said, and meant it. As difficult as it would be to see him on a regular basis, I wouldn't ever shut him out. We were now connected forever by this child I was carrying, *our child*, and I wasn't going to make anything difficult for him—no matter how painful it was for *me* to make an arrangement with him work.

His gaze slid over to the dining table with my soup and crackers. "Did I interrupt your dinner?"

"It's okay," I assured him. "I haven't had much of an appetite lately." And not knowing why he was here was adding to the queasy sensation in my stomach.

"Are you feeling okay?" He looked at my face, a concerned frown furrowing his brows. "Is everything okay with the baby?"

His genuine concern, for both me and the baby, made a huge lump form in my throat. "We're both fine," I managed to say, and knowing I wasn't going to last long without crying—because this entire situation sucked and my hormones were all out of whack—I jumped right to the point. "Jase, can we just talk about what you came here for and get it over with? I'm really tired and—"

"I came here for you," he interrupted me. "And our baby."

For a moment, a silly hope surged through me, until logic intervened and made me more cautious. "What do you mean?" I asked, eyeing him warily.

"It means, I'm here because I want you, and this baby, in my life."

I shook my head in confusion. "I already told you this baby would be in your life, in any way you want. That hasn't changed."

"That's good to know, because I plan to be a hands-on dad," he said, right before his eyes went dark and serious. "What about you, Kendall? Will you be in my life, in any way I want?"

I blinked at him. "Are you…propositioning me?"

He laughed, the sound husky and low. "I guess I am, because I *need* you in my life, so damn much that I'm lost without you in it."

As I tried to process his words, he reached out and brushed a stray strand of hair off my cheek that had escaped my ponytail, the touch so tender and affectionate my heart squeezed tight.

"Jase…I don't understand." My voice shook.

"Let's go sit down in the other room and I'll explain."

He extended his hand toward me and

waited for me to make the next move and trust him, which was so easy to do. Had been from the very beginning. I placed my fingers in his palm and let him lead me into the living room, where we both sat on the couch.

"I have to say, you shocked the hell out of me when you told me you were pregnant," he said, his tone a bit gruff. "And you never gave me a fair chance to digest the news. You just assumed you knew how I'd react, and you pushed me away before I even had time to realize that *we* were having a baby together."

I could feel my face flush and glanced away, knowing I'd put him at an unfair disadvantage that day. "I know. And I'm sorry. The way I handled things was wrong. I was just so scared and afraid…"

He touched his fingers to my chin to turn my face back toward him. "Don't you think I feel the exact same way? Having a baby right now isn't at all what I had planned, but I'm not willing to let you go, and I'm going to be a full-time father to this baby."

The last thing I wanted was for him to feel morally bound to take care of me and the child.

"You don't need to feel obligated to either one of us."

"Obligation has nothing to do with it. Love does." His gaze softened with the emotion. "I love you, Kendall Shaw."

The truth of his declaration was etched on his features. Elation was like an adrenaline rush through my system, and it stole my ability to speak.

He went on determinedly. "The moment you walked out of my house, I knew letting you go was the biggest mistake I ever made. I was fucking miserable without you, but I was convinced that it was for the best, that I'd never be able to give you what you wanted and needed. And then, when I found out you were pregnant, it literally shook up everything I'd planned since I was eighteen, and it took me a few days to wrap my mind around that huge, life-altering change that went against every-thing I swore I would do, until I knew for certain that I was ready for a family and all the responsibilities that went with it."

I managed a nod but let him continue, sensing he had more to say.

"I told you about my parents and how I

grew up feeling like I was in the way and I never had my parents' attention in any way that mattered. They were much older, and spending time with a child who had been an unwanted accident wasn't a priority for them, and I swore I wouldn't make that same mistake with my kids. That I'd be at a point in my life where I was stable and financially secure, so I could make sure that my wife and kids were a priority."

He took my face in his hands, his thumbs gliding softly over my cheeks as he stared deeply into my eyes. "But this baby made me realize that there isn't always a perfect time to get married and have a family. That I'm not giving up anything, or straying from my ideals, but that my timeline has just moved up by a few years and I'm honestly happy about that, because it means I get to spend the rest of my life loving you and all those kids we're going to have."

He pressed our foreheads together, his lips mere inches away from mine. "I hope I'm not too late to be that man for you, that I haven't screwed everything up to the point that you don't want or need me anymore."

"Jase, I will always want you and need you, and so will this child, because we love you and you're the most amazing man I've ever known. *I* love you," I said, because it was important he heard the words and believed them. "We're going to be the family you never had."

He closed his eyes and groaned, as if I'd given him a rare and precious gift. When he opened them again, his gaze blazed with emotion. "Marry me, Kendall," he said fiercely, possessively. "The sooner, the better."

I laughed, feeling incredibly light and happy. "You're going to make an honest woman out of me?"

"Damn straight," he said, his deep growl seductive and deliciously aggressive. "I'm going to put a ring on your finger and make you *mine*."

I suddenly felt hot and breathless, and I leaned forward and playfully nipped at his bottom lip. "How about you make me yours right now, and we'll worry about a ring later."

His eyes flared with the kind of dark hunger my body completely responded to and had missed so much. In the next instant, he pulled me across his lap so that I was straddling his thighs. Framing my face in his hands, he brought my mouth to his and sank his tongue deep. He kissed me slowly, thoroughly, as if I meant everything to him.

When he finally lifted his head, the adoration in his gaze made me melt. The heat and desire prompted me to pull my top off and toss it aside. I hadn't been wearing a bra, and his eyes lowered to my breasts, taking in how full they were now that I was pregnant, how much darker my nipples were.

Very gently, he cupped the heavy weight in his hands and lightly swept his thumbs across the tight tips. I closed my eyes and moaned as pleasure and a bit of pain mingled.

"Are they sore?" he asked curiously, as he continued feathering his fingers over my tingling nipples.

I nodded. "Yes. Very tender."

He swept his hands up my bare back and pulled my chest closer. "Let me make them feel better," he murmured, and lowered his head, his wet tongue licking across my aching nipple before drawing me into the velvet warmth of his mouth.

The need inside me grew, and I shoved my

hands into his thick hair, torn between pushing more of my breast into his mouth and pulling his head away from my sensitive nipples. I rocked my hips against his, feeling the hard length of him beneath the fly of his jeans. I was suddenly desperate for more friction, more pressure, but he pulled his mouth away and looked up at me, his own features etched with equal desire and need.

"Stand up and take off the rest of your clothes," he said huskily. "I want to see you naked."

I moved off his lap and shimmied out of my sweatpants and panties, and his greedy gaze roamed over my body, from my face all the way down to my toes, then back up again. Settling his hands on my hips, he drew me forward and placed a soft, gentle kiss on my stomach, which was still flat but wouldn't be for long.

"I can't wait to see my baby growing in your belly," he whispered reverently against my stomach. "To feel it move and kick. I hope it's a little girl who's as beautiful as her mother."

My heart swelled with gratitude and bliss. I'd never anticipated Jase, or this baby, but I knew this was just the beginning of the life I'd always envisioned. With a man who was everything I'd ever wanted for a husband, and a father to my children.

I shivered as his hand skimmed up my thigh and his fingers delved between my legs, gliding along the soft, wet folds of my sex. I was sensitive there, too, and it only took a few strokes for me to feel the slow, steady rise of an orgasm. Closing my eyes, I rocked my hips against his hand, and when he brushed his thumb across my clit, I felt my knees start to buckle.

He caught me and eased me down to the couch. He stood for a moment to strip off all his clothes, and then he was moving over me, settling between my spread thighs with the thick head of his cock poised at my entrance. Taking my hands, he pulled them over my head and laced our fingers together so that his body pinned mine to the sofa. His gaze locked on mine, and with a slow, steady thrust of his hips, he sank deep and didn't stop there.

He made love to me, slow and deliciously sweet, the connection between us seductive and sublime. Stroke after stroke, he drew out the pleasure, making it last and overloading my senses with the amazing feel of his cock sliding inside me without a condom, the masculine scent of his skin filling my breath, the strength of his body moving over mine—until the building tension and passion finally released and sent us both tumbling over the edge together.

He didn't move off of me right away, but he was careful not to put his full weight on top of me. His face was buried against my neck, and it took him a while to finally lift his head and look down at me. The raw emotion in his gaze made my heart flutter; the smile curving his sexy mouth made me feel like the luckiest woman alive.

"You feel so damn good," he said, his expression content in a way that went beyond sexual. "Like everything that has been missing in my life and everything I never expected to have."

I understood completely, because this man owned me in a way no other ever had. My heart, my body, and my soul.

. . .

Don't miss Stephanie and Mac's story, up next in PLAYING HIS WAY.

Don't miss The Marriage Diaries featuring Dean and Jillian!

To learn more about Erika Wilde and her upcoming releases, sign up for her newsletter HERE.